THE MASTER IS COMING . . . AGAIN

Nosferatu means "the undead." It was the name given to Count Dracula by F. W. Murnau in his revolutionary silent film, *Nosferatu* (1922), the first movie version of Bram Stoker's classic novel, DRACULA (1897). And it is the name given the lonely vampyre with the restless nighttime thirst in Werner Herzog's chilling new film, here captured unforgettably by outstanding novelist, Paul Monette.

The story begins when Jonathan Harker, a blissfully married young real estate agent, is sent abroad to close a deal with a mysterious count. One storm-tossed night, the new landowner arrives on a ship with twelve coffins of dirt and the dead captain lashed to the wheel. Soon the entire town is gripped by plague and Dracula begins to insinuate himself into the consciousness of Lucy, Jonathan's beautiful wife.

Nosferatu is both seducer and seduced in the moving and terrifying climax to the story. Each night he returns to the living. Each morning he returns to the grave. But this time he finds the one bed he cannot leave before the first light of dawn.

NOSFERATU
THE VAMPYRE

A novel by PAUL MONETTE
Based on WERNER HERZOG's screenplay

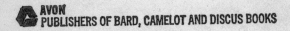
AVON
PUBLISHERS OF BARD, CAMELOT AND DISCUS BOOKS

AVON BOOKS
A division of
The Hearst Corporation
959 Eighth Avenue
New York, New York 10019

First Avon Printing, March, 1979

AVON TRADEMARK REG. U.S. PAT. OFF. AND IN
OTHER COUNTRIES, MARCA REGISTRADA, HECHO EN
U.S.A.

Printed in the U.S.A.

To Gregg and Charlie

one

One

IT was 1850 in Wismar, and nothing was out of place, and nothing ever went wrong. Everything was done in its own time. The cobbled streets were washed at dawn. The lamps were lit at the stroke of dusk. So many flowers were set out at the windows, so many trees rooted outside the old stone houses, that the summer seemed to linger in the squares and narrow streets long after the first chill strangled the country all around. The local stone was the color of honey, as if the town were touched with a vein of gold. The linen hung out to dry above the clear canals was pale as beaten cream. The rose of daybreak and the rose of sunset framed Wismar like a painting. Nothing was wanted from anywhere else. A man would have been mad to have wanted to leave.

"I promise you," Jonathan Harker told his wife on the day they married, "our life will be as happy as a dream."

And he took her home to a sunny house with a chestnut tree in front and a great bay window above the canal. The swans came by in twos and threes, and Lucy Harker turned to watch them every afternoon, while she sat at her embroidery. Her life had turned out just as she had meant it to. She had set her heart on Jonathan years before, when they were still in school, and she'd known even then that all she had to do was wait. A person's life was set to be blessed or cursed from the very beginning, and she always knew that hers was destined to be perfect. Now she was Jonathan Harker's wife, and by and by she would come to be the mother of his children. She kept a house as clean and sweet as the dunes that fronted the sea a half mile off. She had a closet full of clothes she'd sewn herself, as fine as any a duchess wore, and she cooked up custard and raisin bread nearly every day, because her husband couldn't ever get enough. She went from room to room a dozen times a day, and everything was always as it should be.

She never dreamed at all, until one night.

"No!" she cried, sitting up in bed. "Take *me!*"

"What is it, my love?" said Jonathan, folding her in his arms. He hastened to reassure her. "It's nothing. It's only a nightmare."

"I saw you," she said, and her voice was more full of sorrow than fear. "You were gone away to another country. You were crouched in bed like an animal, and you couldn't stop him."

"Who?"

"I don't know," she said. For a moment she looked at him like a stranger, as if he knew and wouldn't tell her. "Why are you going away?"

"But I'm *not*. I told you," he said, and he smoothed her long dark hair against the moonlit lace of her nightgown, "I'll never leave you at all. Not for an hour."

And they fell asleep in each other's arms, and in the morning she could have sworn it hadn't happened. They sat in the oak-walled dining room, velvet cushions on their chairs, and she poured him tea and buttered his toast. Eat more, she told him. She didn't

8

even want him bringing it up, so she chatted to fill the time. It was as if, in dreaming something dark, she'd made a mistake that was better forgotten. Her skin was white as a swan, and her black eyes shone with purpose as she maneuvered the silver service neatly and spooned him out a dollop of jam. She determined to set aside time, before another day was out, to count her blessings. She had had a kind of vision of how life went for people who weren't as lucky as she.

God have mercy, she thought, licking the butter off her thumb, *on those who are not safe.*

Just off the marketplace, with an old stone water trough in front, was an unremarkable, flat-front building that housed the offices of Renfield and Company. A flock of doves was having a morning bath before the premises opened. Renfield, the most successful estate agent in all Wismar, had enough money now to rent himself quarters as grand as the mayor's, but he hadn't the inclination. He liked the feel of the old place far too well, and to him it was a good-luck charm. Besides, he didn't spend half as much time as he used to behind his desk. He'd come to put such trust in his manager, Jonathan Harker, that he lately found himself staying home till nearly noon, where he worked on his beloved collections, butterflies and stamps.

So it was odd to see him out so early, walking through the market, keys in hand. Short and overfed and ordinary looking, he paused here and there at a stall to give an approving poke to a fish or a fat melon. The market vendors tipped their caps and wished him well, and altogether he felt himself a pillar of the town. But even *he* couldn't figure out what had stirred him out of bed at dawn, impatient to be the first in the office.

He was only twenty or thirty feet from the turn to the Renfield building when he had a sudden urge to count his money. He paused in the street and pulled a leather pouch from his pocket. He jingled the gold into his shaking hand and added it up as fast as he could, afraid there was something missing. He got so flustered he had to start over.

At just that moment, the doves scattered in a panic from the water trough, as if they'd been sprayed with buckshot. But there wasn't a sound except the beat of heavy wings as a great black bird settled down into the little square in front of Renfield's office. It had in its beak an envelope sealed with a bold-red drop of wax. And it wasn't so careless as to drop it. It walked along the windowsill and peered inside, as if it meant to deliver the document face to face. But when it saw there was no one about, it contented itself to drop the letter on the doorsill.

Then it flapped its wings and wheeled up out of the courtyard. Just as it reached the roof, a pair of doves was swooping back to finish their morning wash in the water trough. The raven crossed their line of flight. It veered for a moment and clamped its beak on the wing of the female dove and sent her spinning down. Then it vanished over the roof and out across the waking countryside.

Renfield came around the corner, stuffing his purse back into his pocket, and the dove fell heavily at his feet. He looked up, bewildered, but there was nothing there. Only a second dove, circling slowly. He ought to poison all of them, he thought. Let this one be a lesson to the rest. And he stepped around the broken body and thrust his key in the lock.

But what was this? He couldn't guess. He wasn't expecting a blessed thing. But he knew, as he picked up the letter with a terrible thrill in his heart, that this was why he'd woken early.

In the morning room, where the sun came streaming in at the bay window, Lucy's cat played with a locket on the Persian carpet, batting it with a paw and leaping after it. When she pounced on it like a clockwork mouse, the lid sprang open, and she jumped back, frightened. Then she edged forward cautiously and poked it. Inside was a miniature of Lucy, a garland of flowers in her hair, a billowing scarf at her long neck. The cat crouched around it, began to purr, and went to sleep.

"No, no, Lucy, I've had enough breakfast," said Jonathan as he marched in from the dining room to fetch his frock coat. It was laying on the center table, where he'd left it the night before when he came home late from work. He saw he had disarranged the display of seashells Lucy had set out prettily on a doily, and he put them back more or less in place as he slipped the coat on. He bent down to scratch the cat behind the ears and grunted with dismay when he saw the locket open. He snatched it up with one hand and swatted the cat with the other, so that she ran for cover beneath the horsehair sofa.

"That cat is a devil," he said as he came back into the dining room, dropping the locket into his watch pocket. "She's here to bring chaos. Why do we need a cat anyway? There hasn't been a mouse in Wismar in a hundred years."

"I wish you'd have an omelet, Jonathan."

"No time," he said, and he picked up his cup and drained his coffee and then leaned down to kiss her.

She held him back and pouted. "You work too hard," she said. "You never sit still long enough for a proper meal. You know what it leads to? Heartburn."

"Heartburn?" he exclaimed, clutching his chest in mock horror. "Oh my God," he laughed, and picked her up from her chair and hugged her close. "Is *that* all we have to worry about? Let's plan to die of heartburn, Lucy, when we're a hundred and ten."

He gave her a long kiss, then held her head on his shoulder and rocked her, as if he had all the time in the world. He looked through the solid rooms of his solid house, out to where the sun dazzled on the canal, and thought: *I don't need anything else.*

They drifted, arm in arm, to the great front door, with its fat brass knob in the shape of a sheep's head. Of course there wasn't a lock. A man's house didn't need a lock in Wismar. Jonathan took his top hat from the hatrack, plumped it rakishly on his head, and bid Lucy goodbye till midday. He left her standing happily in the doorway, a hand raised to wish him well. The chestnut tree bathed her in a green and yellow light, and he held the image in his head as he turned away, as clearly as the image in the locket.

He picked up his stride when he neared the end of the street, but not because he was hurried. The clear air of the summer morning fairly made him dance. He loved the line of the houses standing straight in a row, just beginning to stir with the new day. Housemaids scrubbed the door stones. Neighbors on horseback called and waved as he went by. The children clustered in groups and sauntered off to summer play. Jonathan felt a proprietary interest in all of it. Something he'd learned from Renfield, perhaps, as if he'd surveyed every scrap of property and had the whole of Wismar committed to memory. But it was more than that. He had a sense of how everything fit together to make a world. The stray and the incoherent, the disjointed and useless—Wismar had ridded itself of all of that. There was nothing that didn't have a place, that didn't go to make it whole. And the whole was as palpable to him today as the shine of the summer morning.

He came out of the street and crossed a bridge, too lost in thought to notice the man in black who stood at the railing. Just a motionless man in black, staring into the water. Nobody in particular, no more than another citizen of a town where people were glad of things in their places. But he looked down at the half dozen yellow leaves below him, floating nowhere on the canal, and couldn't begin to say what he thought.

Passing jauntily through the busy streets, Jonathan came around the corner and into the Central Square. He stopped at a market vendor he'd patronized for years, from the time he was a boy with a couple of coins a week to spend. He gave the man a friendly greeting and chose a pastry layered with cream and frosted up with chocolate. As he walked along and ate it up, he noticed that the shades in the windows along the square were all pulled down to just the same level, as if the council had passed a law. A pair of workmen painted the white picket fence around the central fountain, though it didn't look in need of it at all. He picked out the early vegetables and berries on the market stands and knew exactly what week of the year they were in, without the aid of his pocket calendar. Nothing ever changed except the seasons.

He had finished the pastry, smacked his lips, and straightened his tie in the window of the bank next door when he turned off the square and into the courtyard where Renfield and Company stood. And he had a sudden pang in the region of his heart. He would have laughed it off and called it a case of Lucy's heartburn, and it hardly lasted a second in any case, except that it left him with the strangest feeling. He put a hand to his billfold, in the inside pocket of his coat, and thought with an anxious shiver: *I have to have more.*

And then it passed, and it seemed so odd that a moment later he scarcely could recall the feeling. He shook it off and went inside. Renfield was already at his desk, so Jonathan hung up his hat and went right to work. He knew exactly where he'd left off the night before, in the middle of drafting a contract for a parcel of grazing land on the shore to the north. Because he was meticulous, his table was organized so as to put all his current projects at his fingertips. Not so the office in which he worked. Thirty years of Renfield paperwork was stacked to the ceiling and bursting out of the cupboards. Renfield never threw a thing away, and he couldn't remember where anything was ten minutes after he tossed it aside. But Jonathan didn't mind. Renfield had a flawless sense of men and their property. Their styles were very far apart, but they'd made a proper balance.

Yet if Renfield had no patience for papers, more often than not putting things on piles before he'd half begun to read them, why was he bent so close today? And why so excited? He was practically panting, Jonathan saw. A man who was usually so cool about other people's land and houses. If Jonathan could have seen over his shoulder, he might have wondered a good deal more. Because the paper in Renfield's hands wasn't in any standard form at all. It was covered with figures and formulae, with symbols very like alchemy. As if it were in code.

"Harker," he said at last, folding the letter and locking it in a drawer. "I have the most exciting news. I think we finally have a buyer for Red Oaks."

"But, Mr. Renfield, someone must have misinformed them. It would take a fortune to bring that place to life again. It's a *ruin*."

"Nevertheless," said Renfield gleefully, never more proud than when he brought off an impossible project, "the buyer says he has a sentimental reason. He considers himself quite lucky to have the chance to live in Wismar. What do you think of that?"

"Well, it's wonderful," Jonathan said, though he hoped he wouldn't have to be the one to show the buyer through. It wasn't fit for an animal to live in.

"It's wonderful, is it?" Renfield fairly shrieked with delight. "Oh, Harker, you can't believe how wonderful it is! Wismar is going to have a *nobleman*!" And he drifted about the cluttered office as if the stacks of papers were princely titles. Jonathan dipped his pen in the well and tried to focus again on his work, but Renfield turned and addressed him, grinning in a way he must have thought avuncular. "But Harker, it all depends on you. I can't trust anyone else."

"Sir?"

"Someone has to carry the deed to the nobleman's house. You would have to be away for several weeks."

"I see," said Jonathan, trying not to show his disappointment. He took his job very seriously. If a man wasn't willing to take a risk, he'd never get anywhere. "Where does the nobleman live?"

"Very, very far," the other answered soberly—as if to test him, somehow. "Across the Carpathian Mountains."

"Oh, but that would take a month, either way," he said. There were limits, after all, beyond which a deal was no longer worth it. "How much can he possibly pay for a house that's falling apart?"

"The commission," Renfield said with a casual air, "would be in the neighborhood of fifteen hundred guilders."

"Oh, my God," the young man gasped. It was triple his yearly salary. "Whoever he is, he must be mad."

"I told you, Harker. He's very sentimental. His heart is set on Wismar."

"Still, it's impossible. Lucy wouldn't hear of it."

"Think of the things you could buy her, Harker. Things she's only dreamed of."

"She——" But all at once he couldn't recall what he wished to say about the things that Lucy wanted. He felt the hungering chill clamp down again around his heart. Jonathan Harker was meant to be a rich man. Now was his chance. And the world was full of beggars who let their chances pass them by.

"I'd buy her a house on the park," he said, almost as if to apologize, though he couldn't remember from moment to moment half the things he thought. He, who had always been so methodical. "And then she could have a carriage all her own. A country place for weekends. She hardly knows what there is out there."

And as he talked, he didn't notice how Renfield's laugh had changed. He thrilled and gloated and quivered with passion. The pitch of it was maniacal.

"Harker, it's only the beginning. To have in Wismar a man so rich and powerful—before he is done, we will all be kings!"

But Jonathan wasn't listening. To quiet the wild beating in his temples, he began to spend the fifteen hundred guilders in his head. A hundred for this, and fifty more for that. He made a little list, and in a minute he'd calmed down enough to stare across at Renfield—who was capering about the office, the laughter now like a fit, throwing up papers from off the stacks till the room was swirling in a blizzard. Jonathan didn't have the words to stop it. He felt they had drifted so far off shore, they were no longer in sight of land. He could only wait out the delirium. And just as suddenly, Renfield was seized with icy calculation, and he turned again to his manager, who sat confused and strained as if his head throbbed with a headache.

"It won't be an easy journey, Harker. It will cost you a lot of sweat, and possibly . . . a good deal more. A man does not come back the same from so far off. But you'll go, won't you?"

"I have to, Mr. Renfield," he said, though he had to stop a moment to remember why. He was half asleep. "It would be a relief to get out of the city for a while. Get away from all the canals that go nowhere but back to themselves again."

He sat still, with a distant smile on his face. He felt very content. Renfield patted his shoulder fondly, then turned to the shelf of books above the fireplace. He took down two or three dusty volumes before he found what he was after. He carried it over to Jonathan's desk, pulled up a chair, and sat beside him. A swirl of dust went up as he turned over the pages. Finding at last the page he desired, he shook Jonathan's shoulder and brought him back from the place where he was deep in thought.

"Here it is, Harker—Transylvania."

Jonathan looked down at a map of the rugged mountains, following Renfield's finger through the forests. He couldn't remember when he had felt so calm.

"Beyond the deepest woods," said Renfield. "A place that civilized men have not yet tamed. You'll have a chance to see the virgin earth. Wolves and bears, and the peasants so backward they still believe in ghosts." He laughed again, but now the laugh was scornful and controlled.

"Should I be frightened?" Jonathan asked with a smile.

"No, no. Once you get to the Count, you will be in the hands of the most respected man in the region. His name will open any door. It's settled. You'll leave today."

"Today?"

"We haven't a moment to lose. I've all the papers ready for you. You go home and pack, and I'll get a map and purse together." He paused to think what else was required, and he drummed his fingers on the dusty book. It was with a great effort that Jonathan spoke up. His tongue was almost numb.

"Mr. Renfield," he said, and his voice was pleading. "I'll go. I know I must. But give me a day to break the news to Lucy. She had a bad dream—"

"Of course, Harker, of course," Renfield spoke indulgently. He seemed to have everyone's best interests at heart. "And, in turn, you will promise me one small thing. You must arrive at the castle after nightfall. The Count is away overseeing his kingdom during the day. He would be offended if you arrived while he was off. You'll remember that, won't you?"

"Oh yes," said Jonathan. *Anything, anything,* he

thought, *but please, I want to go home now.* "You haven't yet told me his name."

"His name?" The hand on Jonathan's shoulder as Renfield stood up dug in like a claw and held. "His name," said Renfield deliriously, as if the stars would wink out one by one to hear it spoken, "is Dracula!"

Lucy couldn't sit still all morning. She thought she could smell a piece of food that had fallen under a table and gone rotten. She searched the kitchen and pantry, down on her hands and knees, but after a while she decided it wasn't a smell at all. She tried to sit in the bay with her needlework, but then she began to feel a draft. She became convinced there was a broken window, and she went from room to room, throwing back the draperies, till she'd looked at every one. But nothing. And then it struck her that there must be a leak in the cellars, water pouring in from the canal, but she had to wait till Jonathan came home, since she found herself unaccountably scared of the dark.

When Jonathan ran in and called her name, she was standing in the bay, the cat in her arms, looking out across the canal to the far fields. She hadn't made the first step to get the noon meal on the table. And she wished she'd told him not to come home to lunch, because she didn't feel like talking now, not at all sure what she'd say.

"Lucy, my love," he announced to her proudly, "will you mind very much being a rich man's wife?"

"Rich or poor," she said quietly, more attentive just now to the cat than to him. "That was the promise."

"You have to *listen*," he begged her, turning her toward him so that the cat leapt out of her arms and skittered away. "Renfield has assigned to me the biggest commission of my career. From now on, we're going to live like kings." And when he started to laugh as he danced her around, she couldn't help but laugh as well. There was nothing the matter with the house, she thought. It was just her imagination. "It's happened very fast, Lucy. I have to leave tomorrow morning."

"Where?" she gasped, and she saw how she'd been tricked.

"A castle," he said. "Off in the Carpathian Mountains." He looked down tenderly into her face. "I have to be gone for a while. And *you* have to be brave"

"You won't come back," she said with an awful resignation.

"Don't be silly. I'll be back before the first leaf falls from the chestnut. That's a promise."

"Don't go," she moaned, laying her head on his shoulder. "Don't go." She was so limp in his arms, he would have thought she's fainted if she hadn't spoken. "We're all in terrible danger," she whispered. "You can stop it now if you stay right here, if you never let me go."

"I won't listen. You're being ridiculous, I tell you." He released her from the circle of his arms and walked around her in a mocking way. He would have said he was trying to lift up her spirits, to get her to laugh at herself, but the words were brittle off his tongue. She felt them as a punishment. "You're as bad as the peasants up in the mountains, Lucy. They hear a wolf, and they're sure it's a ghost. But when was the last time somebody heard a ghost in Wismar? We got rid of them long ago, along with the rats. Now come and help me pack."

And he went away through the sitting room, looked at his letters as he passed through the study, and bounded up the stairs to their bedroom. He pulled down his saddlebag and heavy pack from a high cupboard. He didn't really have to get ready till morning, but he felt somehow that Lucy had to be made to face it now. She acted like a child. He rooted through a trunk for his riding clothes. He took the trees from his finest boots. Then he went into the closet under the eaves and found his leather hat and his rough woolen cape. He was just coming out of the dark and into the light of the bedroom again. He had to squint against the sunlight at the windows. But he suddenly stopped as if struck dumb, and his mouth dropped open and made no cry.

A thousand leaves were raining outside his windows. Chestnut leaves, bright green with summer. They came so fast, it seemed that someone had to be pouring them off the roof. He knew they couldn't come from any tree. The bedroom faced the canal, and the chestnut trees were out in front, lining the quiet summer street.

"Lucy!"

She had just reached the top of the stairs, and she hurried in. He gazed at her now with a look of terrible doubt. She knew exactly what it was. He was anguished over the tone he had taken a minute before, and right away she forgave him. She walked to him bravely—just as she knew he wished her to—and smoothed the tension from his face with a touch of her fingertips on his cheek.

"Of course you'll come back," she said gently, keeping the tightest grip on the terror still inside her. And he darted his eyes to the window, where the sun came through and made the gauzy curtains glow, the floorboards shine. "But come," she continued. "Today you belong to me alone, and I want to go walking on the beach. I'll find a shell to bring you luck."

"You are all the luck I need," he replied. With an arm around her shoulders, he left the gear for his journey strewn about the room. As they went away downstairs, he put what he had seen out of his mind entirely. It was nothing but a trick of light. He couldn't afford the shock of superstition. He swore he would do this thing like a logical man. The mountains, the wolves, the castle at dusk—none of them any more than a problem to be solved. He needed only a glance at the row of chestnuts along the street to know that things were still in place. The real world was the only one that Jonathan Harker believed in.

The tide was out, and they walked along the hard, flat sand, just at the point where the rippling waves were spent. The sky was growing gray in the afternoon wind that had sprung up out of nowhere, just as it always did in May and June. The sky was aswirl with gulls who rode and swooped. Lucy and Jonathan were free and unencumbered, feeling the way they did whenever they came here. There were forces reeling all about them on the beach—the wind and the sea and the distance—but they saw it all as a universe of laws. They'd fallen in love while walking here. Here, one night with the moon on the sea, was the place where Jonathan first proposed. They would have shared it gladly with anyone who wanted it. There was room on the long miles of sand for ten times as many as lived in Wismar. In some way, though, it was theirs alone, and only they two knew it.

"I will come here every day," she told him fervently, clinging close as the wind whipped the billows of her white silk dress. "I'll look out over the sea, and my blessings will surround you. Whenever you think of me, you will be as safe as you are in my arms."

"And what shall *I* do," he asked her gallantly. "I'll find our star in the sky each night, and make a wish. I'll wish—"

"Don't tell me."

"I'll wish to be safe in your arms again," he finished, putting a finger up to her lips, not about to be stopped by another superstition. "And you know what? I wouldn't be surprised to learn there are other creatures, far away on other worlds, who look up in the sky and wish on us. Because we're charmed, you know."

And at that, they reached the point of land where the fir trees came to the water's edge. This was the very spot where their earliest passion flowered. They came in under the shadow of the sighing boughs, and the wind died down. They sank into the bed of soft and fallen needles. They embraced. In a moment they kissed with the fever of secret lovers.

She felt it still like a sickness—nameless, deadly —but she had no choice. Before all things, she owed him the duty of a proper wife. She clung to her vow of obedience. She prayed that the rightness of things would save her. But even now, at the pitch of love, as her body floated in the harbor of his touch, she felt the deadness waiting on the other side. Each of his kisses would end before the day was out. She began to count them, every time she met his open mouth with hers, as if she were counting the strokes of a clock on the way to a catastrophic appointment.

But at least *he* didn't know. He lay in her arms and thought himself the happiest man in the world. It was a victory none of the forces of evil could take from her. For this one hour, she fashioned around them an image of perfect love. She fixed it in her mind so she'd never forget, no matter what intervened. *I'm a king,* he murmured in her ear. And so he was, for this one hour.

There was a group of five or six around him when Jonathan mounted and rode away.

He had the idea that it would be easier on Lucy if there were others about to distract her once he was out of sight. He paid a call on Schrader, Lucy's brother, late in the evening after they'd returned from walking on the beach. He made Schrader promise to look in on Lucy, to keep her busy and calm her fears, and they worked out the plan for a picnic in the stable yard out behind Schrader's house, along the wide canal. Jonathan could easily slip away in the midst of a celebration.

Mina, Schrader's wife, had laid enough food for twenty. Steaming fish chowder and shepherd's pie. A ham and a turkey. Renfield came, and Dr. van Helsing was pulled in off the street as he left a patient in the house opposite. Then the seamstress who'd been sewing Mina's clothes was called down. And the stable boy who was readying Harker's horse. It was *almost* a party by the time that Jonathan and Lucy arrived.

Lucy had her wits about her. The visions had gone away by the time she'd come back from the beach the night before. The nightmare didn't return, but then she hardly slept. She lay in bed by Jonathan's side, clutching the pearl gray shell she'd taken from the water's edge. She looked at Jonathan sleeping and told herself that love was all the answer that she knew. When she helped him pack his gear in the morning, she'd begun to hope again. If the love between them was true as she knew it to be, then it ought to be able to bear the test of distance.

At the picnic, she went from one to the other, full of warmth and ease. The motley group that Schrader and Mina had gathered at the last minute seemed, when Lucy passed among them, close and friendly as any family. She could feel her husband looking across at her with pride, and she determined he would ride off full of relief on her account.

"Schrader," Jonathan said to his brother-in-law, "Lucy is the dearest thing in the world to me. And nothing will keep me from coming back to her. Not death itself."

23

It was time for him to go, but he decided to wait till she'd eaten a bit, who was always feeding him and never thought enough of herself. He called her name across the yard, and she turned with a radiant smile.

"What will you have to eat, my love?" he asked, gesturing toward the plentiful table under the trees.

She followed his pointing finger and screamed. A rat was crawling out of the turkey. Another was burrowing into a loaf of bread.

They rushed to her side, and she tried to tell them, but of course there was nothing there. Dr. van Helsing told Jonathan to go. They might as well get it over with. Mina and the doctor held her up as her husband bent to kiss her one last time, but she felt as if she were being tied down, and she snarled and broke away. Jonathan drew back as she advanced.

"Whatever it is just laughs at us," she said. "It cannot help but win."

"Go," said the doctor. "Go," said Schrader. And Jonathan backed away in a daze, till the stable boy put the reins in his hand. Lucy stood in a fury twenty feet away. She had given up the final kiss.

"I see it more clearly than ever," she said. "It is a shadow that creeps across the ground. Gigantic. Grasping. Everything it touches dies."

"Go," they said, and Jonathan mounted. The others clustered around him and swore it would be all right when he'd finally gone. He turned in the saddle and waved to her, but she would not come any closer. She put her head in her hands and wept.

He rode away. The others looked down at the ground, ashamed at having witnessed it. All but Renfield. He looked across at Lucy weeping, and he grinned from ear to ear.

24

Two

IT took him two days to cross the coastal plain, then another three to make his way up through the foothills. And during all that time, he suffered to think that he'd left poor Lucy in such a state of desolation. He struggled every hour with the thought of turning back. The summer heat on the flatland made him despair. The sight of every closely nestled town, of every happy couple walking in the fields or on the road, struck him with a pang of what he'd left behind. He wrote her letters every time he stopped his horse to water, and he folded them up and gave them to coachmen and drivers of herds, whoever he met who was going as far as Wismar. For the first five days, he was still a townsman, and the wild outdoors and open country had no meaning for him. All the good of the world seemed concentrated far away, in a house from which he was riding father and farther off in the wrong direction.

But then a curious thing began to happen. The logical man inside him started to be interested in the foreign details of the changing landscape. The plants and rocks, the brittle soil, the moths and earthworms—everything was new, and he spied them out with a cataloger's eyes. He began to clip leaves and peel off bits of bark. He took samples of soil as he mounted up higher and higher. He tapped away a fragment of stone from any rock formation he couldn't readily identify. Though he'd scarcely paid attention to Lucy's shells and Renfield's drawers of butterflies, he found to his delight that he was a secret naturalist. As he went along into the mountain wilderness, he discerned an order in things as profound as any system in the tidy world of Wismar. The ache of missing Lucy never stopped, but it didn't keep him from searching out the mystery and loveliness that burgeoned here on every side.

It was midday, some time into the second week. He was deep in the Carpathians by now, and the country was increasingly rough and stormy, the steep trail unpredictable. Coming down a twisted path with the woods on either hand, he came to a brook where he let the weary horse drink. He slid down out of the saddle, shook the dust from his cloak, and knelt to the stream to wet a kerchief and bathe his face. His eye was caught by a stark, enormous tree that must have been split by a stroke of lightening.

It rose up fifty or sixty feet, the bark all fallen off, and the scar at the core was black as sin. And he realized as never before how vast the scope of violence was. It wasn't just a broken twig, or a dead bird dashed in the path. There was power enough to shake the world to bits. He forced his mind to run to the mechanics of the matter, trying to measure the voltage of the jolt or gauge how long before the tree fell over. But it was no use. He saw that he couldn't hold everything in his hand and figure it out and put it in place. There was a magnitude of things that no man yet had fathomed. There were no instruments in existence with which to do the measuring.

And the farther up he rode into the mountains, the more he became aware of a split in things. There were beautiful, fragile moments everywhere—spider webs wet with the dew and weeds with blossoms as bright as roses. But then there were ruinous landslides, and strangled trees where a blight had hit, and the torn-up carcass of a deer. He couldn't work out the proportion. He couldn't decide why the nature of things was one way here, the other way there. He heard the howl of wolves in the night, and he knew they were only wolves, but it didn't quell the shrinking in his heart. While the wilderness had lured him on with a promise of form and a thousand flawless unities, now it told him the rest of the story and showed him chaos bare.

The second week passed, and then the third. He began to throw off the manners of a townsman's life. He didn't bother with the tin cup in his saddlebag when he stopped to drink. He leaned down and gulped at the stream along with his horse. He spied out the berries the birds most favored and tore them off the bushes and ate them in bunches. He rode in the heat of the day with his shirt off, and his skin grew tough and dark. Though he'd made up his bed quite neatly at first, on a cushion of leaves, now he slept on the bare earth easily, a fire going all night long to keep the wolves away. The landscape hardened every day, and the evidence of violence grew, but he was stronger and wilder himself as he traveled on. He met the brute world face to face.

One night when he was very weary, he came through a narrow pass between two crags and onto a level space lit up by a bonfire. A group of children dressed in rags came running forward to cheer him on. It was a gypsy camp. Jonathan hadn't seen another human face in well over a week, not a single rider on the trail, and he was overcome now with brotherly feelings. The sight of tents and donkeys and people at work called him back from his brooding solitude. He dismounted and made his way to the group that was seated at the fire. He didn't even remember that gypsies were barred from entering Wismar, on pain of imprisonment. If he had remembered, still he would not have been able to say why. There was no particular reason, in fact. It was simply a given that renegades and good-for-nothing types had no place in a world of laws.

Jonathan sat among them now and tried to tell them who he was, but he found to his dismay that they spoke a strange tongue. He had to be content with being grinned at and fussed over. There were maybe fifteen or twenty in the group, and they vied with each other to see how hospitable they could be. They fed him stew that he scooped up greedily with wedges of coarse black bread. They passed the wine to him over and over, and he learned to squirt it out of a goatskin into his mouth. But the feeling of being an alien persisted, though they sang to him and played a drum and fiddle to make him laugh.

When the dinner was done, and the songs and dances, the women and children gone off to the tents to sleep, he stayed at the fire with half a dozen men and attempting once again to tell his story. He made miming motions in the air of drawing up a deed. He drew a map in the dirt with a stick. "Wismar, Wismar," he told them again and again. They nodded and smiled encouragement, hugely entertained, but he knew they hadn't a clue what he meant. He pointed off into the unknown reaches and tried to describe a castle with his hands. He spoke the words automatically, to accompany himself, but of course they didn't hear. Until he said "Dracula."

He might just as well have drawn a gun. They froze in horror. Then fell all over each other scrambling away. He didn't know what he'd said to offend them, but he felt awkward and ashamed. He heard them moving from tent to tent, and they whispered the news to everyone. It came back to his ears like a kind of chant: *Nosferatu, Nosferatu!* How had he hurt them? What local god had he trampled on? He could only sit and wait. If they'd just come back, he'd find a way to apologize. They mustn't be frightened of *him*.

And finally, after the whispering died away, a single man came out of the shadows, quaking with terror but coming ahead with his arms extended. In one hand was the polished blackwood fiddle. In the other he clutched a mass of jewelry, strings of amber beads, and silver ropes and buckles. He came as close to Jonathan as he dared, then crouched and laid the offering at his feet. Jonathan didn't know what to do. He sat in shameful silence as the gypsy ran away. He supposed he would only make it worse if he tried to follow. He stared at the fire till it died to a glow and prayed it would all be better in the morning.

But when he woke in the misty dawn, he was all alone. The clearing in the rocks was empty. The caravan had gathered up when he fell asleep and moved off without making a sound. He leaned up on one elbow and saw his horse cropping the meager grass, all unconcerned. The fiddle and jewels were still heaped up next to his pack, and a rolled-up rug. He didn't see how he had room for any of it, but he couldn't just leave it either. He stood up and stretched and turned around.

Behind him, just at his head while he slept, someone had driven a crude white cross into the ground. He hadn't heard a thing, but that was not why he shivered now. It reminded him of something else. A marker on a grave.

Lucy couldn't say how long it had been since she had

slept. She lay in bed exhausted, night after night, but something held her back from the luxury of going under. It was fear of the dream, she thought at first. Surely she would go mad if she had to see Jonathan caught again, cowering in bed like an animal as the horror advanced to claim him. But gradually, as she began to live with this endless waking, she had the sense of a growing purpose. She dared not yield to anything. That was just what it wanted. If she should let go in any way—if she slept, or swooned, or even turned her attention to some detail and so forgot to watch—she would be lost. She had to keep it like a vigil, though she didn't know why.

Yet she knew she wasn't doing it for Jonathan. She prayed for his safety and pledged her love till the end of the world, but she also knew he was on his own. This other thing that she couldn't name and couldn't see, that had made her throw away the comfort of sleep, was to do with her alone. She walked the beach by the hour, and Mina would follow behind and try to get her to talk of boats and sea birds. Schrader gathered her up each night and brought her home to a sumptuous dinner, where the talk was always merry and everyone told her how lovely she was. She went along so they wouldn't get angry and get in her way, but she didn't pay any mind to any of it. She nodded and smiled politely. All the while, she kept this secret space in her head, blank and clear like a cloudless sky. And she waited.

Imperceptibly, she began to look at Wismar in a whole new way. Staring into the public garden one long afternoon, she found the flowers all too straight, the hedges too neatly trimmed. When she stood alone in the market square, the prosperous merchants looked to her like so many puppet figures chiming the hours on a clock. Nobody ever stopped to think. And she drifted along the canals and saw the vast production going on at every house—the baking, the meals, the sweeping and washing, furniture going up and down stairs, and round after round of deliveries. Everything aimlessly going forward. And this, she thought, was why it was coming. None of these petty, distracted people would ever be able to stop it.

She didn't know what to do. She hadn't a soul to tell it to. Unless she talked to Renfield.

She didn't like him at all. He treated Jonathan like a servant, and he affected a proprietary air with her that made her cool and tight-lipped. But he was the only one she could trace the beginning of her feelings to. If Jonathan hadn't had to take the journey, none of this horror would ever have started. She didn't know what she planned to ask Renfield, and she certainly wouldn't reveal to him all she'd figured out. But she dressed in a rose-colored tea gown, looked at herself in the mirror for the first time since her husband left, and brushed and ribboned her hair. If she only showed him a little kindness, surely he'd agree to help her. And why not give him the kiss she knew he craved? He'd do anything then. He'd probably turn the nightmare off like a faucet.

With a parasol twirling over her shoulder, she went through the town to the market square. And all along the canals, they said that Lucy Harker was looking better at last. They knew she would come to her senses by and by. She crossed the market and turned into the little courtyard of Renfield and Company, but in a moment she found that the door was locked. The dust and disarray inside told her the office probably hadn't been open since Jonathan left. As if the business Jonathan had in his pouch were all the business the company had.

But Lucy was undaunted. She made her way through narrow streets to the oldest quarter of the town. When she came to Renfield's gate, she saw she was in luck. He was darting around the sunny yard, butterfly net in hand. She could do it all in the garden, she thought. She didn't need to steel herself to the musty reaches of his house. She called his name as prettily as she could, and he waved hello but held his finger up to tell her to wait. He was on the trail of a red-winged beauty, and just this moment it lighted on a yellow tulip.

He stalked it, stealthy as a panther. Net in the air, he moved by inches toward the tulip. He really was a very harmless man, she thought. Eccentric, full of humor. She began to think he would have an answer to all of her fears. With surprising speed, he brought the net down over the flower and gave out a whoop. He grinned at Lucy the grin that never seemed to leave his face.

"Cupraxis narcissima," he announced triumphantly.

"Let me in, Mr. Renfield," she called, rattling the gate with a white-gloved hand.

He bent to the net, put his hand under, and brought out the crimson butterfly. He held it by the body between finger and thumb, and the wings flailed uselessly, trying to fly away. Now don't be squeamish, she told herself. It was a very scientific hobby. Besides, she needed him too much right now to put him off with shuddering.

"Bring it to me, Mr. Renfield. Let me see how pretty."

He sailed his hand back and forth in the air, as if he were letting it fly again, and his laugh went higher and higher until it was empty air. Then he brought his fingers up close to his face, as if he meant to study it minutely. But he opened his mouth and stuffed it in. And chewed it like a cracker as he came toward the gate.

It was evening in the Carpathians. The valley was high up, with the peaks of jagged mountains all around it. It had been raining for a month, and it was going to rain again, but just now the sky was heavy with clouds, the rain biding its sullen time. A muddy road wound its way through the pass and trailed along the valley to a weatherbeaten rural inn. The only glimmer of civilization in three days' journey through the steepest country. A mail coach drawn by four tired horses approached along the way, and it was clear the coachman was a single-minded man determined to arrive before the fall of dark. He didn't have a minute to spare.

Next to the inn was an open blacksmith's shop, with the forge aglow as the smith repaired a carriage. In the meadow beyond, a pair of chestnut horses chased in the high green mountain grass. As the coach came to a stop in front of the inn's wide porch, the bearded coachman unwrapped from around himself a thick Tartar rug. He climbed down and rapped on the coach door to announce their arrival, just as the innkeeper came outside.

"I see you've gone into horse-trading now," he said, pointing to the roan tethered at the back of the coach.

"Nothing so lucky," the coachman said. "I picked up a passenger on the road. He'll stay the night."

"You mean a guest?" asked the gray-faced innkeeper, wiping his hands on his apron, patting his tangled hair. There hadn't been a guest since the previous summer. Or was it the summer before? He stepped up smartly to the door of the coach and flung it open. "Sir or Madam," he announced with a low bow, "welcome to Traveler's Rest."

Jonathan squinted out sleepily into the dusk and stepped down to the muddy yard. He was stiff from the ride, and he'd adopted something of the coachman's laconic attitude. The innkeeper chattered behind him as he lifted down Jonathan's gear, trying to express how proud they were to have a distinguished foreign visitor. Jonathan let him talk, without any sense, as he would have felt in Wismar, that he had to be pleasant in return. He called a rough greeting to the blacksmith and demanded that his horse, lame in the left hind foot, be given special care, and he sauntered into the inn.

The candlelight and open fire were welcome sights. He ordered a port from the innkeeper's wife and went to stand on the hearth next to the coachman. The rough-beamed room in front of them was cluttered with heavy wooden tables and benches. The smell of fat was strong, as if it seeped from the walls. Hunched over at one table was a group of four peasants, playing at a game of cards so slowly you couldn't detect a motion. A woman sat on a bench, a covered basket on her lap. An exhausted goose kept poking its head out, but she thrust it back in each time. Nearby, a dull boy picked his nose.

"Who *are* all these people?" Jonathan asked the coachman. "Travelers?"

"Not likely," the other answered, draining his port and calling for another. "I told you, nobody travels this far back in the Carpathians. These are the poor folk whom God has doomed to live at the end of the world. I don't know what they do. A little farming, though I can't imagine what grows *here*. Mostly, they get in a lot of accidents, and they kill each other for sport."

"I see," said Jonathan, holding out his mug while the innkeeper's wife poured from a stone jug. A few more peasants straggled in and found their tables. They seemed accustomed to take their supper here, as if it were the only bright spot in their day. Godforsaken they certainly were. They limped and crouched, and one had an empty socket where an eye was gouged. A poor thin woman appeared to have the palsy. Various of them coughed as if they would expire before the food reached the table.

Jonathan thanked his stars that his luck was better. When his horse went lame the day before, stumbling in the fog on the bumpy road, he thought he'd be lost for weeks before he came out on foot. But just as he made ready to leave his horse and all his goods to seek help, the mail coach happened by. The coachman agreed to take in payment the brass bowl and the gypsy rug to carry him to this lonely spot—as near as Jonathan could tell from the map, the place where the main trail through the mountains forked with the road to the castle of the Count.

The coachman was too tired to eat, and he swore besides that the inn served swill. So he brought a whole jug of port for himself and repaired to a room upstairs, leaving Jonathan the object of all the curious staring in the room. Bacon and potatoes and strong mountain wine were brought in great bowls for the peasants' table, but the innkeeper laid a cloth for Jonathan, setting it out with a knife and napkin and a jar of wild blue flowers. Jonathan sat and waited, staring at his plate, the noise of the poor folk eating coming to his ear like the sound of a barnyard.

The innkeeper laid down a plate of steaming food —a kind of meat and potato pie—and spooned out a portion. Jonathan shuddered at the sour gamy smell, but he had to eat, as the innkeeper stood by expectantly. Jonathan smiled to show his delight, though his stomach turned. And the hard-luck peasants watched his every bite, envy in their eyes.

"You are a hiker, sir?" asked the innkeeper. "You have come to climb a mountain and put up a flag?"

"No," he said. "I have business hereabouts."

The people around him at the other tables snickered at the mere idea, and the innkeeper laughed out loud.

"But sir, there *is* no 'hereabouts.' All you see around you here is all there is. We have no 'business' in the mountains."

"Innkeeper," Jonathan said disdainfully, "you show yourself a fool. We are not five miles off from the castle of Count Dracula. I hope to say *he* has business enough to keep him busy."

In a flash, the room was as still as death. Then a sudden crash. Jonathan looked up and saw that the innkeeper's wife had dropped a stack of dishes on the floor and clapped her hand to her mouth in horror. The dimwitted boy began to choke, and the grizzled man next to him slammed him on the back till he coughed it up. Jonathan peered around, and he saw two or three make the sign of the cross and move their lips in prayer. There was such fear on the faces as he had never seen. He'd seen many a man fear death, but this was something else.

"I beg you, sir," whispered the innkeeper. "Must you really go so far?"

"Indeed I must," said Jonathan coldly. They were really very transparent, he thought. They were scared of money and power, and the only comfort they had in their ugly lives was the fond belief that the castle was haunted. Otherwise, of course, they might have gnashed their teeth at so much inequity. The gulf between a count and a ragged cripple would have been insupportable.

"You won't find anyone who'll take you *there*," called the girl with the goose.

"I'll go on my own horse, thank you," he said. "He likes a ghost as much as I do."

"Your horse needs a good week's rest," said the farrier. "And you won't rent another in *this* valley."

"I'll *walk*," snapped Jonathan.

While they talked, the palsied woman crept up behind him, a rosary and cross in her gnarled hand. She touched his shoulder, and when he turned, she slipped it around his neck and clasped it. He wanted to take it off and hurl it, to prove the point more forcefully, but the pity in her eyes stopped him.

"Well then," she said, "may God have mercy on your soul."

"I was a miner in these parts," interrupted one of the men who was bent at the card table. When Jonathan looked over, he saw the man was blind and staring straight in front of him. "I was out collecting samples. I wandered across his boundary by mistake. I saw—" and his face went blank as he tried to see it again, "I can't remember what I saw. I ran and ran, and I somehow made my way back here. Young man," he cried, "why can't you understand? We are the ones who *escaped*!"

And he let the silence tell the story of all of those who hadn't.

But Jonathan thought they must be having a joke at his expense. He had come too far, had braved too many solitary nights on the trail and emerged unscathed, to fall just short of his goal for fear of ghosts. It was a matter of pride, as much as anything.

"When I ride back through this sorry place," he announced to the room as he stood up, "I will stop by for a glass of wine. Because I am a gentleman, I will toast the health of Dracula, the ruler of these regions. I wonder who will drink with me."

And with that, he stormed away from the fireside and took the steps to his room two at a time. He shut the door and stood against it and breathed a sigh. He couldn't help but feel a little cheated, naturally. He'd rather hoped for an idyllic mountain village nestled outside the castle walls. He'd pictured country folk who lived in harmony with nature on the one hand, the lord of the manor on the other, passing their days in wholesome work and loving comradeship. These warped and brokenhearted people at the inn could only make him sympathize with the isolated nobleman who wished to move to Wismar. He would tell him so tomorrow, in fact. No wonder the Count wanted people arriving after dark. If a man thought he'd come too late to intrude, he might end up spending a night in this luckless inn.

The room was simply furnished and oddly crooked, as if the building had started to sink. The bed was atop a dais, as was the custom in Transylvania, and the legs were so high that a man could not climb into it without the aid of a stool. Otherwise, there was a simple desk and chair, a dresser with a bowl and pitcher, and a bootjack on the floor. Under the bed, a chamberpot. Jonathan hadn't been in a room in more than three weeks, and he felt a creeping sense of unease at being ordered about by furniture again. On his journey he had slept wherever he fell at the end of the day. He washed when his face was hot and sweaty. Relieved himself against the nearest tree. He resisted the comfort and cleanliness here. If it didn't mean his passing down among the peasants yet again, he'd go outside with his woolen cape and sleep in the open.

A knock on the door. It was one of them come to apologize, no doubt, for trying to scare him like a child. But it was only the innkeeper's wife, who begged him to let her turn down the bed. He shrugged and sat on the dainty chair to take off his boots. She watched him carefully all the while she worked, fluffing the pillows and pulling out the eiderdown from the chest at the foot of the bed. As he struggled to pull his second boot, she took a book from her apron pocket and laid it down among the newspapers next to his candle. Then he turned and opened the window and took a deep breath of the night air, and she revealed a vial of holy water in her hand. She unstoppered it and shook the drops on the pillow.

"May God protect you," she said, modestly withdrawing to the door.

"I protect myself as best I can, madam," he said. He did not turn from the window. "May God protect the poor dumb beasts of the field. They need it more than I."

She closed the door behind her, and he wondered, as he stripped out of his riding clothes, why he'd sounded quite so unrepentant. Of course he believed in God and hoped for heavenly protection. But he couldn't help but find this continual business of blessing just a trifle tiresome. It seemed no better than any other superstition when they started up with the crosses and the holy invocations. All of that was better left to Sunday, Jonathan thought as he climbed up into the bed and tried to get himself settled among too many cushions.

He was about to blow out the candle when the leatherbound book in the flickering light caught his eye. Or the title did. In bright gold letters across the cover, it glimmered up at him: *The Undead.* In spite of himself, he picked it up and flipped to the index. He mumbled the phrases over to himself.

"Vampires and bloodsuckers. Corpses devouring their flesh. Incubus and succubus. The living dead." He smiled. He was hardly interested at all, to begin with, but he began to enjoy the sound of the ghoulish phrases rolling off his tongue like an incantation. He thumbed to the center of the book and read out: "Werewolves. Beware the full of the moon, when all the axes shall be milked of blood." Whatever *that* meant. It was comical, really. He turned over another block of pages. And his eye picked up the word he'd quite forgotten: *Nosferatu.*

"Nosferatu," he read aloud, "the Undead. For all the unspeakable sins of man was this creature born, to wreak revenge upon the parents, children, children's children, unto the last generation. The curse will last until the end of time. The curse of the vampire, *Nosferatu."*

And suddenly, out of nowhere, a roaring sound like a whirlwind began to swell in the room. Jonathan looked to the window, but though it was open, the curtains hung still, and the night outside was motionless under the gloom of clouds. The gust of wind blew the newspapers off the table and rippled across the eiderdown. It ruffled his hair like an angry hand. It blew against him so that he had to shut his eyes against the force. And then it snuffed the candle out, and the room was still.

In his confusion, Jonathan had the irrational urge to shut the window, still telling himself the storm had come from without. He climbed down out of the bed and went and parted the curtains. As he reached for the latch of the open casement, the somber gibbous moon groped its way out of the clouds. He looked up at it now as if he'd never seen it before. It was a planet newborn in the mountains tonight. And then the howling began in the crags around the valley. Horrible, drawn-out, plaintive, wronged. All through the darkened inn, Jonathan could feel the frightened people sign the cross on their pounding hearts.

Then the moon disappeared as quickly as it came, and Jonathan looked out as if hypnotized. From a hundred places up and down the valley, he made out the flash of yellow eyes glowing. The howling grew and grew. And without thinking what made him do it, Jonathan opened his mouth and let out a lonely wail. He howled back at the sorrowing creatures of the night. The horses in the stable below kicked against the walls in terror. Jonathan joined the wolves in the cry they made, louder and louder, and he felt a delirious sense of relief. For a moment in the window, his eyes gleamed yellow, and he saw a vision of darkness deeper than the night. And then he slumped to the floor.

The morning dawned clear and bright. The horrors of the night had all withdrawn to their lairs. When the first ray of the sun struck Jonathan's sleeping face, he twisted as if it scalded him and woke with a start. He groaned as he sat up on the floor. He had hardly slept at all, it seemed. He began to dress, but he couldn't shake the feeling of an unutterable weariness. How many hours before the night, he wondered, longing to rest again.

He was turning to the door with his pack in hand when the book caught his eye among the pillows. He didn't want to remember it. He wished he hadn't ever seen it. But he picked it up and stuffed it in a pocket of his pack. And he spied among his things a prize that lifted his spirits—the silver pendant with Lucy's portrait tucked inside. He pulled it out and flicked the cover and gazed at the one he loved beyond all else, and he felt his strength returning. He pinned it into the folds of his homespun shirt, close to his heart, and clattered down the stairs, ravenous for breakfast.

The innkeeper and his wife served him with eyes downcast. The peasants who entered the inn, when they saw him, turned on their heels and went out again. Only the coachman, who'd slept through it all, greeted him heartily when he came down. Laying a necklace of gypsy silver on the table between them, Jonathan asked if he could travel by coach as far as the fork to the castle. The coachman shrugged and scooped up the loot. For this kind of payment, he didn't ask questions.

When Jonathan was finally settled in the coach, he determined not to think about the people in the inn again. But he couldn't help but notice the innkeeper whispering to the coachman, and the latter's start of fear. A milkmaid stood nearby, looking gravely in at the coach window, and making the sign of the cross over and over. The innkeeper's wife shook out a dropper of water at each of the wheels. It was really like an asylum for the mad, Jonathan thought, his pride rising up again. He called the coachman roughly and buried himself in his cloak.

What was this *longing* he couldn't shake? As the coach wound up the narrow track, going higher and higher, the horses plodding heavily, he had this sense of *craving*. But though the hunger beat like a pang in his heart, he couldn't say what it was he wanted. He had always been a man who *had* what he wanted.

Buzzards circled above the coach. The trees were like cadavers, and the few leaves they flung out were like a pitiful offering for which they would be whipped by a greedy tyrant. The remains of the winter snow still clung to the stems of the shivering flowers. The coachman whipped the horses' flanks, driving them forward mercilessly. They snorted and steamed, and now the fear seemed to have reached them too. But the high country where they were passing seemed to go on and on. They would never reach the end of this.

And when they stopped at the head of the pass, the silence was like dying. Jonathan climbed out, shaken and sick, and he looked about at the heaps of ice-cracked stones, the shredded flags of mountaineers. He saw the fork in the trail, and the road he had to take swooped down into a forest dark with grief.

"Please don't leave me," he whispered, turning to face the coachman.

"Hurry, man," the other cried, as if he were strangling in the suffocating air, "get out your pack and go!" The horses strained to move on. "We are late. The sun is sinking. I must be out of the Borgo Pass before the sun has set."

"But listen," Jonathan pleaded. "I'll pay you twice again as much if you take me as far as the castle. I'm ill. I can't be left alone."

The coachman jumped down from his seat, tore open the door, and hauled out Jonathan's pack. There was pity in his eyes as he handed it over. He had grown quite fond of Jonathan.

"I would ask you to flee this cursed land with me," he said, "but I fear you would not go. Whatever it is you have come to find, you cannot turn aside from it now. I have no advice to help you. A man does the best he can, I hope."

And shaking his head with sorrow, he climbed up

again and flicked his whip and flew off without a backward glance. Jonathan stood frozen till the coach was only a speck, rounding the bends as it hastened away. He hadn't been able to speak when the coachman gave his final warning. Something wailed in his head like a wounded animal, begging him to leave, but he couldn't say it and couldn't move. And now that he could, he picked up his gear and took the fork down the ashen road. When he tried to think of the coachman, to try to figure what he had meant, he could hardly recall a feature of his face. Twenty paces down the road, the sunlight dimming with every passing minute, he couldn't imagine what had happened to the day. A moment ago, he'd been eating breakfast. But if you asked him where, he couldn't have said.

He crossed a foaming brook, where the spring thaw raged, on a footbridge made of stone. At the near end was a statue of a man in prayer. At the far end someone had smashed a statue till it was rubble. There was no way of knowing what it once depicted. He had crossed a kind of border, he supposed, but his mind was dull. The shadows were so deep in the woods he'd entered, he only wanted to give it all up and sleep, right in the path. If he hadn't had Renfield's warning spurring him on, to make sure he arrived at the castle just at nightfall, he would have stopped and waited for the night to come to him. He had a feeling it would hold him like an angel.

But then he began to notice the shadow he cast on the ground as he went. Deeper than all the darkness settling in the trees, and waving as if it had wings. He could hear a kind of whistling in the air, and the whirring of a thousand creatures flying. He tried to run away from the image he seemed to cast, and it only grew more grotesque. When he looked to the sky, as if to beseech it, he saw the clouds go racing, just as the sun had all day long. Everything fled this place but him. The night was in his heart.

And then, far ahead on the path, a strange and phantom carriage came toward him. A glass coach meant for burials. It was drawn by four black horses, funeral cloaks draped across their backs, and it made no sound as it approached. It came on so close that Jonathan thought he'd be trampled—silently, though, with no noise but his screaming. Fire flew out of the horses' nostrils, and their eyes were tranced and glazed. The coachman—wasn't there once a coachman who took care of him?—wore a black cloak with a wide collar that hid his face. Low on his forehead he sported a musketeer's hat with a long black feather.

He turned to beckon Jonathan in, and a stray gleam of light must have touched his eyes, because they glowed for a moment like the eyes of a jungle cat. But though he strained to see, Jonathan couldn't make him out. He tried to speak, to apologize for the shadow he cast, to say the darkness was all his fault. But he knew he must climb in. The world of words was over. He settled back. He couldn't remember what it was he was meant to do when he got there, but he was sure it would change his life forever. A comet veered in the night sky. Yellow eyes sparkled at the wayside. And Jonathan Harker had the strangest feeling that he was going home.

She woke up screaming. But it must have been a dream, because there wasn't a sound in the room, though her jaws were open and she'd clutched the quilt so tightly in her fingers that the edge was shredded and spilling feathers. It was still the middle of the night, but Lucy knew she wouldn't sleep again. She'd broken her pledge to stay awake forever if she had to, but she decided she had to face the dream and force herself to the other side of it. She couldn't stand the waiting anymore. But though she prayed herself to sleep each night, she woke in the middle to find she'd had no dreams at all.

44

But there *was* a sound. A whirring by the window, in the folds of the curtain. She struck a match and lit the lamp, and the commotion turned to a fury as something tried to release itself. Lucy rose from the bed. This could be it at last. She picked up the lamp to go forward and expose it, and the curtain billowed out. A bat flew a circle round the room.

"I *know* you," Lucy said in a savage voice, but she couldn't imagine what she meant. The words came shuddering out of her, as if from a dream she couldn't recall.

The bat was trying to get out, but the light had made it blind. She set the lamp down on the table. She threw open the cupboard door and caught up a broom. She ran toward it, beating the air. It was just a bat. It lived in the eaves of a windmill across the canal. But she cornered it and knocked it down. She hammered it with the broom again and again. When it was dead, she staggered back and fell on the bed. She was panting. She lay on her side and buried her head in the pillow. The desire that fountained up in her body was so intense, she thought she'd scream.

Three

THEY came to the gate of a castle deep in the woods, its towers lost in the night clouds. The iron gate creaked up, and the glass coach drove through into the courtyard. The hooves and wheels were deadly silent on the cobblestones. The coach stopped, and the door to the coach opened, as if a ghostly footman danced attendance. *There are no ghosts,* Jonathan told himself numbly, climbing out. He stood in front of a great stone portico, with vast black doors so tall and heavy he knew he could never open them, even if someone bid him enter. He turned to ask the phantom coachman what to do, but the coach was gone like all his dreams. His pack was beside him on the pavement. The gate was down. The castle had sealed itself like a tomb, and he had no gypsy silver left to buy his passage out.

He never would have knocked. He would have stood there frozen forever, like the statue of a man who could no longer pray. But he wasn't required to have a will of his own. Slowly, very slowly, the doors swung open. From the darkness beyond, a figure began to approach, so rigid it seemed to have come through a region of ice to reach him. He was wrapped in a tight-fitting black cape. His shoulders were hunched, and his hands were cramped together at his chest, one on top of the other, as if he didn't dare to let them swing free at his sides. Jonathan couldn't bear to look, but it didn't matter what he couldn't bear. He had slumped down onto one knee, to keep from fainting, and his wide eyes stared ahead at the terrible hands. Long and bloodless, limp and slightly quivering by turns, they tapered into nails as horned and yellow as claws. But even if they meant to clamp his neck and choke him, Jonathan forced himself to accept the creature's hands. To welcome them, almost. If only he didn't have to look up into the face.

But he had to. He tilted his head and raised his eyes and saw. The face was as white as the underbelly of a slug, inching its life away under a rock. The head was completely bald and bulbous like a skull. The ears were twice the size of a man's, flared and some-how twitching, as if the only nerves in all this deathly body were concentrated here, listening frantically into the darkness. The lips were puffed like double bruises. But oh, the eyes. They were sunken in, and they spoke of pain that laughed at time like a cruel joke. The slightest glance from eyes like these could lay a town to waste. They had never blinked. Had never cried.

"Dracula?"

"Yes," he sighed, in a voice that ached with desolation. "I have been expecting you, Jonathan Harker. The air is very thin up here. Let me help you up. You must lean on me till your strength comes back."

And he glided forward, light like a shadow. Jonathan scrambled to his feet. He knew he would rather die than touch this man.

"I'll be all right," he said. "The dizziness has passed. It's just—could I have a glass of water?"

"Thirsty?" asked the Count. "Of course. I have had

a supper laid out for you. You have only to put yourself in my hands. You cannot know how happy it
make me to have a guest whom I can serve."

He turned and took a burning candle from a nook
in the wall, and he lit the way down the vaulted corridor. Jonathan carried his pack on his shoulder, and he
felt the great doors shut behind him as he followed.
For a moment Dracula held the candle close against
his cloak. Jonathan could have sworn he saw the light
through the other's body, as if the Count were no more
substantial than a curtain billowing at an open window. But the image fled as quickly as it came. He
couldn't keep his mind on anything long enough to
work it out. There was nothing to fear in a man this
sad, he told himself. The corridor stretched before
them like a tunnel into another world, but now he was
here at his journey's end, so he must be safe at last.
It was a relief, after so many weeks on the lonely
trail, to have someone to follow.

At length the corridor opened into an immense
room lit by madly dancing candles. The high windows
were covered with grates like a dungeon. The walls
were swathed in tapestries. The mouth of the fireplace
opened twice as tall as a man, and the timbers burned
like hell itself. The massive table in front of it had
chairs enough lined up on either side to seat a hundred people. But a hundred people drunk and laughing, breaking bread together, could not have dispelled
the sense of chill and sickness. An ironwork chest at
the hearth, where Jonathan laid down his pack,
looked as if it hadn't been opened in centuries, yet he
was sure he heard the faintest scratching at the lid, as
if whatever it was had never ceased pleading to be
released. Though the head of the table was richly laid
with food, it gave no hint of nourishment. Hunger
would not be satisfied here. The thought of food made
his stomach shiver. But Dracula drew out the chair,
and there was nothing to do but sit down.

"But won't you join me?" he asked politely, noticing only one plate, one mug.

"Ah, no," said Dracula gently, taking the chair to Jonathan's right. "I am a lonely man with lonely habits, Jonathan Harker. I take my food on the stroke of midnight. But you will permit me to serve you, I hope. The servants are not just now at our disposal."

And the clawed, attenuated fingers pulled the joint from a roasted pheasant and dropped it on the plate. Then he plucked some grapes from a bowl of fruit. Cut him a slab of goat cheese. And he poured him water in a crystal glass and filled his mug to the rim with wine, and Jonathan watched in a trance as if they were the motions of a priest. But he had to overcome a sense of nausea before he could take a bite, as if the food were rotten. As if there were something more he needed, except he couldn't say what. He swallowed water. He ate the soft inside of the bread. And in a moment he'd come to himself again. He began to eat with greater relish. He mustn't forget who he was, he thought.

"You have some papers for me?" Dracula asked.

"Why, yes," he said, laying down his fork. "They're in the pocket of my pack. I'll get them for you right away."

"No, no. You sit and eat. I'll find them.

But somehow it made Jonathan nervous to see the Count bent over his pack. He was looking for something else. The roll of documents was clearly visible, right at his hand, but he rooted through the pack with a restless desperation. He must have realized he had gone too far. He snatched the roll of Renfield's papers and stood up, taking a deep breath to compose himself before he turned around. Jonathan stared into his plate, not knowing what to do. What of his did Dracula want?

"Eat, eat," urged the Count, pacing back and forth

as he unfurled the plan of the ruined house in Wismar.

Jonathan lifted a forkful of game. He chewed and chewed and got no taste. He had never had such a perplexity of appetites before. How long did he have to stay? he wondered. A yes or no from Dracula—wasn't that all he needed? He'd be back with Lucy in three weeks' time. Then he could savor life again like any other man. He had no wish beyond that—to be just like everyone else again. Then he would no longer have this feeling that a stranger buttered his bread and chewed his food. He couldn't help but feel that here, high up in the mountains, Dracula was more real than he was. Wait till they both lived in Wismar, he thought. Then they would see who fit and who didn't.

He heard a clock begin to strike, and he turned to where it hung on the wall. Dracula was already riveted, quaking as he listened. He had his cloak clutched about him, and the documents lay on the floor. On the face of the clock, a miniature skeleton sounded the hour by beating on an anvil with a tiny hammer. At the twelfth stroke, a small door opened, and a figure in a shroud appeared with a sickle. He sliced the air once, mechanically. It was only meaningless little joke, thought Jonathan, who could no longer comprehend what had become of time. And then he heard the howling of wolves start up outside the castle, and he shrank against his chair.

"Listen!" exclaimed the Count. "The children of the night have taken up their music!" And he let out a high laugh of triumph and threw open his arms. The cape billowed in the air like wings. He turned, and the look of inexplicable pleasure on his face was such that Jonathan clamped his hands to his mouth to keep from screaming. "Jonathan Harker, you shake with fear," said Dracula with an angry pride. "You cannot place yourself in the soul of a hunter. You are as

51

puny as all the mountain villagers, and fate will sweep you away!"

Jonathan tried to act as if nothing had happened. Dracula stood in the firelight, looking as if he meant to strangle every living thing. He was just another madman, Jonathan told himself, reaching across for a piece of bread. That is why they had a madhouse, even in Wismar. Sad and lonely people ended up losing their minds. But he wouldn't listen to raving, he thought, cutting a piece of cheese. He knew the mad were harmless, and they only hurt themselves. The silence built like a dare between them. Jonathan determined not to look at the Count till he'd finished his dinner. He put the bread and cheese together and cut it in two.

And the knife slipped and sank into his thumb. The blood bloomed like a flower.

"Oh, look!" Dracula moaned in a low voice. He was at Jonathan's side in an instant, taking hold of the wrist. His jaw dropped open slackly, and he bent toward the wound. But the terror in Jonathan's eyes, the pulling away in disgust, seemed to bring him up short. He forced himself to let go. He stepped back a pace. With a shudder of nerves, his arms crossed at his belly as if he would have a convulsion, and he began to talk brokenly.

"The knife is very old," he argued. "If it has a vein of rust—the blood can boil with poison, Jonathan Harker. I have seen men beg to die. If I draw it out. If I—suck the blood before it taints. It is the oldest remedy in the world, you understand."

"It's nothing," Jonathan said, binding his napkin around his thumb. "It's a surface wound. In a moment it will close by itself."

But the blood came sparkling through the linen. The cut was just a little deeper than he thought. Dracula held back, and the torment that racked his face revealed a struggle as dark as warring angels. He made as if to turn away, with a terrible effort of will, but his left hand fluttered out from his body like a winged creature disembodied. He appeared to have no control of it as it gripped the other man's wrist again. He opened his mouth as if to plead with his own satanic fingers, and yet again he lost control. The upper lip curled back against two jagged teeth. Swiftly he bent to Jonathan's hand and tore the napkin off with his teeth. His mouth covered the wound as he fell against the table.

For a space of seconds the two were motionless, fixed together like stars in a constellation. Then the vampire sprang away as if beaten off, appalled by his loss of control.

"You—you do understand," said Dracula, rubbing his hands together in a chafing way. "It's the only way to avoid infection."

Jonathan staggered up from his chair, but he didn't know where to turn. He couldn't recall the way out. He was too weak to fight. He backed against the edge of the fireplace, the horror crawling over his skin like the beat of insects, and for a moment the despair reached such a pitch in his heart that he thought he would throw himself into the flames, because the nightmare was not going to stop now—ever.

But he reeled forward and sank onto the chest, clutching his pack for dear life. He groped his way back to himself again, like climbing a cliff face hand over hand. He blanked everything else from his mind except the will to see the world as real.

"Sir," he said in a voice without inflection, "I believe we have business to discuss."

"Not now," said Dracula, strange and distracted, as if he had too much else on his mind. "You are exhausted from your journey, Jonathan Harker. Wait till you've had a day or two of rest. There will be time enough for worldly matters then."

"I would like to conclude the arrangements," Jonathan gasped. His guts were churning with nausea, and he couldn't focus. "Please—if you sign the papers in the morning, I can be on my way."

"In the *evening*," Dracula said, coming closer and peering at Jonathan, who had pillowed his head against his pack and now moaned softly, clutching his stomach. "I am away at the crack of dawn, and I don't return till the fall of twilight. That will be soon enough, I hope."

"As you wish, sir," Jonathan whispered. "I think— I must sleep now."

"Of course, of course."

There was something more that Jonathan wanted to say, something he was terribly sorry for. He felt his limbs going numb as if he'd been drugged. Only a minute ago, he thought deliriously, he had committed some kind of crime. But he couldn't remember now. He swooned and went under, and the last sensation that gripped his heart was guilt. He was in a state of sin, and he didn't even know what it was.

He woke to the hollow sound of a gypsy fiddle, and for a moment he thought he was back in the mountains, safe in the gypsy camp. He was lying on the ancient chest, his arms folded across his chest as if someone had measured him for a coffin. He sat up and looked about, recalling where he was with a kind of dull indifference. By day, the dining hall seemed much, much smaller. Its neglected, shabby character was evident throughout. The motheaten tapestries, the cobwebs swooping at every corner, all the furniture cracked and leaning—everything gave the impression that the castle hadn't been inhabited for decades.

He yawned and shook off the shroud of sleep. He examined the cut on his thumb, but it seemed to be well on its way to healing. He stood up and felt a sudden throbbing at his neck. He felt the spot with his fingers. Two small welts very close together, as if two gnats had nestled down on his skin to mate. Not painful, really, but very sensitive to the touch. He looked around for a mirror, so he could study it rationally. But there was nothing bright enough in the general gloom to give him back his reflection.

Then he noticed the table was laid afresh with food, and he forgot the irritation on his neck as he fell to eating. He couldn't be bothered putting things on a plate. He ate with his hands, stuffing his mouth and chewing with a happy concentration. He was scooping up a pudding with his fingers when he heard the skirl of the fiddle again. The sound was coming in at the high barred window, but he couldn't see out unless he got a ladder. He wandered away from the table, wiping his hands on his shirt. He went through a door at the end of the room, down a narrow passage like a tunnel, and came out into a circular hall where doors opened off in every direction. He walked to one at random, opened it and went in. It was a bay-windowed chamber very like another he'd known, but so long ago he couldn't remember.

On the bed was a pack and saddlebags, a woolen cloak and hat. He was sure they belonged to someone he used to know, but it slipped his mind just now. He crawled up onto the window seat and threw the casement open. He gasped and clung to the ledge, because the drop to the courtyard below was thirty or forty feet at least. But he leaned out into the gray and windy air. He'd caught sight of a ragged boy sitting on a moss-covered balustrade above the tortured garden, playing a lonely song on his fiddle.

"Boy!" called Jonathan. He was so elated to see another human face. It had been so long he couldn't say. "Tell me, please, what is this place?"

But the boy didn't notice, or he couldn't hear him. Jonathan shouted and whistled. The lonely song went on. When it ended, the boy stood up and made his disconsolate way downstairs to the garden, and in a moment he went out of sight. Jonathan pleaded till he was hoarse. He felt as if he'd watched his own youth vanish. He fell back in on the window seat and put a hand to his heart, which throbbed with longing for a time that was no more. But his fingertips touched the locket pinned inside his shirt, and he drew it out as if it might contain a clue. He'd never seen it before.

And when he clicked it open and saw her face, the wreath of flowers in her hair, the white neck like a swan, the whole of life came flooding back. Lucy! He looked up gratefully, and the tears came hot and free. He saw the gear on the bed and knew it as his own. The room he was in was the replica of the room they shared in Wismar. The color of the drapes, the china horses on the bedside table, the needlepoint cushions on the bed—all precisely the same as the details of the room above the canal! It should have made him shriek like a man falling, but Jonathan Harker smiled. How kind of the Count, he thought, to set it all up to remind him of home. The Count didn't want him forgetting who he was at all.

He looked at Lucy's face till he thought he'd burst with joy. Then he pinned it in place again in his shirt and moved off dreamily out of the room. He didn't appear to feel any fear at being in the castle. He found a passageway that circled all around it, with slit windows every fifty feet or so, to protect the place from its enemies. Every time he reached an exit, he found it locked. But instead of making him feel trapped, each successive discovery only made him feel more secure. At one point he opened an inner door and found himself in the library. Bookstacks rose to the ceiling, full of thousands of faded, dusty volumes. The silence lay so thick about that it was clear the room had not been entered in years and years. Just as well, Jonathan thought. You couldn't believe what you read in books.

And when at last he came again to the dining room, he climbed up onto the table and sat cross-legged. He ate and ate, till he fell over laughing to think a man could eat so much. His belly ached, and he fell asleep in the midst of his meal. He could hear the gypsy boy's song, fiddling in at the window, and it seemed to him, as he drowsed on the table, that the Count had ordered a song to make him think of home.

Mina came by at one o'clock, as usual, to set out something for Lucy's lunch. If she didn't, the poor girl went all day without a bite. She called a greeting, and Lucy only murmured in reply. Mina knew she was sitting in the bay, surrounded by all the books she'd borrowed from Doctor van Helsing. Morbid books about insomnia and madness, apparitions and the evil eye. She had drawn her beautiful hair up into a bun, and she wore a gray dress and jacket as drab as a schoolgirl's. She was pleasant to everyone who called on her, but regretted every invitation. It was spoiled and shameful behavior, Mina thought, and reflected poorly on a town where a woman's duty began with looking pretty. If she didn't watch out, her husband would decline to take her back when he came home. Mina almost wished it would be so, as an object lesson to everyone.

"Lucy," she called, "I've put out a lovely potato soup, with a pat of butter in it. Come and eat it while it's hot."

Lucy drifted into the dining room, a close-printed book held up to her eyes. She propped it up on a candlestick and sat at her plate. Mina saw that she didn't bother with her napkin. And she didn't notice that Mina had chosen the Celadon soup-plate, to go with the vase of dogwood brought from Mina's garden. She didn't notice the dogwood, either.

"It says here, Mina, that in the Middle Ages, if a man had a vision involving a bat, he was put to death, and his body was buried far out at sea. Now why was that? Why didn't they try to find out what it was really a vision *of*?"

"I'm sure I don't know," said Mina primly. "People having visions don't belong in nice society. Eat your soup."

Lucy lifted the spoon to her mouth and swallowed. Immediately, she was struck with a terrible sense of pressure in her stomach, as if she'd gorged herself. She clenched her teeth and dipped the spoon in the soup again. If she ate another bite, she was sure she would explode. Food was a kind of torture. But she swallowed again and kept on eating. And though her eyes had hardened, and the cords in her neck were taut with pain, Mina didn't see what she was going through at all. That was the test of Lucy's strength.

She'd been attacked for the last two days by a series of disorders, every time she ate—nausea, satiety, thirst so bad her lips had cracked, one thing after another. But she knew it was only the beginning. She had to use these minor agonies now to toughen herself for the horrors ahead. She hadn't seen a vision in a week that took the shape of a rat, as if the power that taunted her out of the darkness knew it didn't strike terror in her anymore. So it twisted a knife in her stomach instead, stabbed and stabbed till she thought she would start to pray to die, but she told herself: *Take one more bite.* And so she inched her way through hell.

"Oh Mina," she said, "you spoil me. I'll have another bowl." In her secret heart, she dared to taunt the darkness back. The fire shook her belly like a prisoner in a dungeon. "This time, Mina, with a double pat of butter."

Jonathan sat at the window in his bedroom, staring out on the falling dusk. He had one hand clasped around the pendant pinned to his shirt, and the other held a stub of pencil at an open diary on his knee. He wore a calm smile and a distant look, as he had all afternoon.

"Lucy, my love," he had written, "it is as if you were with me now. I cannot tell you how, but I am sitting here in our room, and I feel you are going to walk through the door at any moment. I can't imagine what life will be like when I return. *You* are the only thing that I can imagine. Tonight I finish negotiations with the Count, and tomorrow I start the journey back, to fly to your side. If you only knew how much you are in this room. . . ."

The last light went in the woods around the castle, and Jonathan shook himself from his reverie and prepared to go into the main salon for dinner. He tucked the diary again into his saddlebags. He pulled out the sheaf of documents from Renfield and Company. He burrowed deep inside the pack for a clean handkerchief, having promised himself to eat his dinner like a gentleman, no matter how fierce his hunger was. He pulled the folded cambric out, and a gleam of something caught his eye. Did he still have a bit of gypsy silver? He burrowed deeper and brought up the rosary hung with the little cross. Now who had given him that? And what did it mean? It was as if he had no associations at all with crosses. But he pinned it around his neck because he thought it made him look prosperous, and he felt the cool of the cross against his heart as he swaggered through the hall and tunnel to join his host.

The Count was pacing nervously, back and forth in front of the fire. He made an impatient motion at Jonathan as soon as he set eyes on him, gesturing him to sit at the table and eat. Jonathan went quietly, sat in his chair, and began to help himself to food. The Count kept pacing, but now he began to speak, and Jonathan had the impression that he meant to bare his soul. Jonathan was flattered to think they had reached the level of confidences. Perhaps they would end by being kinsmen.

"I don't attach any importance to sunshine anymore," said Dracula. "I am no longer interested in the fountains of day, where a youth stands dreaming, throwing in pennies. I love the darkness and the shadows, Harker, because they let me be alone with all my thoughts. I am the descendant of an ancient family, which has lived for hundreds of years in this . . . house." He smiled for a moment as if at a private joke, and he looked up into the shadows of the high and vaulted ceiling. "I am the last of the line, and my heart is the resting place, the *guardian*, really, of all those centuries. Time to me is an endless cave that has no entrance on the surface of the earth. You understand? The centuries come and go, and still one cannot grow old. Death is not the only end, you know. There are things more horrible still." His ears were flattened against his bulbous skull. His pasty lips quivered with pain. He groped the air with his hands, to try to find the words. "A man cannot even imagine it, Harker. Enduring year after endless year, experiencing each day the same futile longing, the same wild hunger!"

And he turned to Jonathan as if he would gather him in his arms. But he saw the astonished look and seemed to understand he had said too much. He let his face go blank again, and when he spoke, the tone of his voice had lowered.

"I spent a long time looking, you know, before I decided on Wismar for my new home. Won't you tell me about it?"

"It is like any other town," Jonathan said, trying to keep the tremor out of his voice. The fear had come back, though he couldn't say what it was in Dracula's incoherent monologue that had called it forth. But he had the most vivid sense that the fear was a friend, that he mustn't let it go. "Everyone keeps very busy. Everything's kept in its place."

"Order is a sign of hope," the Count remarked. "I'm sure it will do me good to be there. And Red Oaks sounds like the perfect house, don't you think?"

"Perhaps. It needs a lot of work."

"Ah, but I plan to work like a demon once I get to Wismar. You have the papers ready?"

"Of course," said Jonathan. He made a move to withdraw the roll of documents out of his shirt, but they caught somehow on the pin of the pendant. It slipped out of the fabric and clattered against the table. Dracula's dark eyes widened. It might have been the twin to a cherished thing he'd had himself, a long, long time ago. His hand shot forward, like an eagle's claw, and he gripped it as if the fate of the world depended on the truth it told. The bony yellow fingernail covered the face of it like a cloud across the moon, and he clicked it open and brought it close.

"But this . . . is what I mean," he said, in a kind of daze. "She has this perfect skin. As if nothing on earth could ever touch her. She is . . ."

". . . my wife," said Jonathan, feeling naked, feeling robbed. "Please, I need it back."

"You call her what?"

"Lucy," he said, and he felt a shiver of betrayal for saying her name at all. Forgive me, he thought. He stood and came around the corner of the table. He advanced on Dracula, who looked more terrible now in his joy than ever he did in grief and pain.

"Of course," said Dracula, something like a smile beginning to twist the rat's flesh of his cheeks. "I've slept so long, I've quite forgotten how to dream. But I always knew it would be . . . Lucy."

As Jonathan gripped his hand, and the Count snarled like a dog and drew away. Jonathan fell against the table, feeling as if he would faint.

"Your hand!" he gasped. The room about him

swarmed with death like a flock of blinded birds. He had never touched a thing so cold. The tips of his fingers burned as if they were infected. And once again he could feel his memory start to slip. The fear flew out of his grasp, and he couldn't recall what it was that so offended him. Something to do with Lucy. Something to do with . . . someone.

"Here," said Dracula, most politely, laying the pendant on the table, closing the lid, as if to bring them both to earth again. "Only show me the place, and I will sign."

"But we haven't discussed the price," protested Jonathan.

"That," said the count, "is a trifle. Between gentlemen, a price is always fair." He drew out a drawer at the end of the table and brought out a pot of ink and a quill. Uncorking the ink, then dipping the pen—why was it that everything he did was like a passage out of a ritual, leading them ever further into the night? He signed his name like a scar across the paper, and Jonathan sensed that something dear to him alone was signed away in the bargain.

"Tell me," Dracula said, as if a plan had come to him only then, "how long did it take you to come from Wismar?"

"Just four weeks."

"Aha. But that is by land. If a man were to go by boat, he would reach the place in half the time. I have always longed to be brought in on the tide. The sea is so uncontrollable, don't you think?"

But before Jonathan could answer, could ask the Count to make his meaning clearer, the clock began to chime again. Jonathan didn't turn, because he dared not look away from Dracula. With every chime, the Count grew more enchanted, as if a vision danced inside him. *Oh God,* thought Jonathan, though the air was deaf to all entreaties now, *let the clock stop.* Too late, too late. It sounded twelve with a fatal relief, as if done with time at last.

And the vampire came toward him, staring at his neck. His arms floated up around him, beating the air like wings. His pact with man was signed and sealed, and he came to claim his kingdom. Jonathan backed away against the table. He grasped at fear like a falling man at the empty air. Sin put its hands around his heart as if to cup a candle's flame in a darkness that had no end. He knew the worst at last: he *wanted* this.

His head lolled on his shoulder, and his mouth went slack and drooled. The vampire stood above him, drawing aside the folds of his shirt. The lips drew back, and the rat's fangs gleamed as the vampire sank against him. The necklace fell just along the ripest beat of the pulse, and the clawed hand came up to rip it away. But at the very moment that he grabbed it, the silver cross revealed itself, glinting as it dangled from the chain. And the vampire moaned like a wolf in the teeth of a trap. He groped away in a rage, and he stood and screamed as if he would crack and tumble the walls of his ancient house around him. As if the whole world had to pay for this one broken promise.

The caped arms flailed in the air. The eyes glowed yellow in their sockets. Jonathan turned to stumble away, and he stepped on a thing that writhed and squealed. He looked down as he ran, and there were rats all over the floor. His feet bumped against them. They flung themselves at the ankles of his boots. He reached the door to the tunnel and turned in terror, to see if the vampire followed. And the vampire stood his ground and screamed, and flung out his hands and flung out rats. They swept in a wave from under his cape. Their hunger would never cease.

Jonathan flew along the tunnel, and when he reached his room, he chained the door and pulled the wardrobe over against it. He yanked the beads from around his neck. He made as if to kiss the cross, but it smelled of a festering wound, and he had to turn his face. He tried to pray, but the words in his throat were strangled so they sounded like the whimper of a dog. He could only clutch it in his hand. He threw himself on the bed and wept that he was ever born.

How many hours had passed, he could not say. But he'd wrung out all the tears he had, and the exhaustion that followed on the end of them had brought with it an eerie calm. He lay against his pillows like a man who'd outlived a fever that laid to waste the country all around him. He was alive, and that was all. In one hand was the cross and chain. In the other, the open pendant holding Lucy's portrait. Moonlight streamed in the window.

He did not know why the vampire had not followed, nor even that the cross was the charm that had thrown him off. Because he feared so much to lose his memory again, he turned to his saddlebag to retrieve the book of legends, to keep his mind alert. He had to put down either the cross or the pendant to fetch the book from the pocket. He let go the cross. Let it slip down the pillow till it hid itself in the fold of the sheet. And he leafed the book open to where he'd left off before life swept him into the nightmare. No mockery in his voice now, he read it aloud like a sentence of doom.

"Nosferatu. Woe unto him who learns his name, for even the quick of life will pale into shadows. Night is the vampire's country. From the seed of Belils is he born, who feeds on blood and lives in tombs. He brings his train of coffins heaped with the soil of graveyards. He crosses the earth and leaves them, one by one. The Black Death reaps his harvest."

Beyond the window he could hear the wolves, baying at the moon with exultation. But the silence lay thick in Dracula's castle, and Jonathan knew the assault of the night was over. The horror had reached such a pitch that it finally left him numb. *I am Jonathan Harker of Wismar,* he thought, making his affirmation of himself against the onslaught. He didn't seem to understand that it didn't appear to be so anymore. He lay in a heap, his hair wild and touched with gray from a thousand frights. His clothes were torn and ragged like a beggar's. A town like Wismar drove from its gates the vagabonds and luckless men. A man was not who he said he was unless he had some proof. The madman, rattling the bars of his cell with his cup, swore he was God till he was hoarse, but no one came to let him out.

The proof lay in his hand. He stared at Lucy's portrait as if it would keep him sane. It was his passport back to the land of the living. He had nothing else left. He once had a dream of order and purpose, driving him on to tame the wildness of the earth. No more. He was content to be nothing else but Jonathan Harker of Wismar, and he sank into sleep with his last belief. The gods were gone, and the power of darkness quivered with lust to own the world, but a man could still be who he was. It was like a last nakedness. It made him feel cleansed and somehow holy.

It was a lie. He was still a man because he was blind, because he could grasp at a grain of hope in the midst of a nightmare. Evil moved in his blindness as if under cover of darkness. Along the blackness of the tunnel, the figure of the vampire was advancing. His face was frozen, his hands in front of him open as if to bless the damned. He had started forward the moment the cross slipped out of Jonathan's fingers. The words of warning from the book of legends beckoned him like a siren's song. He reached the door of Jonathan's room, and it swung open slowly as if a ghost preceded the vampire and cleared the way like a footman. The heavy wardrobe wedged on the other side fell over without a sound.

The vampire reached the bed of the sleeping man, who was lost in the dream of the final delusion, that he was still who he was. The vampire picked the pendant out of his hand as if he were plucking a flower. He came down on Jonathan, covering him like a cloud. The rat's mouth clamped against the neck, and the teeth sank in. A stillness deeper than death was upon the face of things. The moonlight went out like a guttering candle. The struggle was all over.

Four

THE night was mild in Wismar. Moonlight flooded Lucy's bedroom. She started awake, as if to flee from a dream, and then she scrambled out of the bed, as if the danger lingered there. She backed away against the wall and stared at the empty bed. Some impossible act of darkness that only she could see appeared to be taking place, and she couldn't stop it. She turned to escape, and she seemed to glide across the room to the window, as if she would float out onto the moonlight. Then, as she looked out to the quiet fields beyond the canal, she smiled with a strange assurance. The terror and danger had fallen away.

She wasn't awake at all. Her eyes were as motionless as the moon, and when she drifted across the room in her nightgown, down the stairs and into the street, she was still as deep asleep as ever. She went like a wraith, a hand above her head waving like a dancer. She seemed to bless each house for the last time, and the distance in her eyes and the haunted smile welled up from the deep place she had prepared to make a stand against the approaching catastrophe. She whirled along a street of shops. She flew to the public garden and capered barefoot around the rim of the fountain. When she came at last to the market square, she waltzed for an hour with the night itself. And there was no fear in Wismar, all the while she danced.

Waking, sleeping, she had taken a kind of command in the town. She was the only one who seemed to want the responsibility, but it only seemed to make her more determined, to know she was all alone. If the others had guessed so much as a fraction of what was to come, they would have despaired and given up. Like Renfield, they would have begun to crack. But Lucy—pure as a virgin, adamant as a saint—saw it all and still believed she had a chance to stop it. No man knew the fire inside her.

She danced till nearly the break of day, till her nightgown fell from her shoulders and she stood naked in the street. She walked across a bridge and made her way down to the bank of the central canal. Like a tightrope walker, she stepped along the old stone wall above the water. She had forgiven Wismar every sin that the nightmare meant to punish and avenge. The moon was down, and in the pearl and violet light of the end of the night, this naked sleeping girl was a promise of a new beginning. She could not help but save them all. And when she did, they would start all over, changed by the awesome purity she brought to their defense.

The distance still in her eyes, the smile in place, she was on her way home to wake in her own bed. She'd passed a mile on the edge of the calm canal, to where the wall followed the border of Schrader's property. And Schrader, restless and ambitious, was already out in his stable yard, hitching his horses up to his wagon. He had a dozen appointments between now and noon. He was taking the feed bags down to the grain bin under the wall when he saw her coming like a ghost. He thought she meant to jump in and drown, and he shouted: "Lucy! No!"

The noise jarred her awake. She was shot through with despair, as if the spell she'd woven over the town would never work if the journey through to the end of the night were interrupted. She raised her hands as if to pray for only a few more moments in the trance, and she didn't seem to understand she was teetering on a wall. She stumbled and fell. Luckily, Schrader had reached the foot of the wall below her, and he caught her in his arms. But even more than he was concerned for her safety, he was shocked and horrified at her nakedness.

"Lucy," he cried, "what have you done?" As if a naked woman walking free were the darkest thing that could happen.

But she couldn't answer. She'd swooned in the course of her fall, and he carried her senseless into his house, shouting to Mina to call the doctor. When Mina appeared, in nightgown and cap, and saw what Lucy had come to, she couldn't help but say to herself that she'd seen it coming for days. She'd always suspected that Lucy was somehow not the same as the other women in Wismar. She'd tried to tell Schrader any number of times, but he wouldn't hear anything spoken against his sister. Now, Mina thought, they would see who was right about Lucy Harker.

They summoned Doctor van Helsing, who hurried along to Schrader's house, frantic to think there was something the matter with the girl he loved like a daughter. The servant girl who'd awakened him brought him up to Mina's room, where Lucy lay unconscious under the anxious gaze of her brother and sister-in-law. They'd covered her up in a robe. They told him what they could about her sleepwalk, but they didn't say a word about her nakedness. The doctor bent to take her pulse, and he felt it race beneath his fingers.

She opened her eyes and stared around, but it was clear to them all she saw no one there. Schrader and the doctor both reached out to restrain her, but she shrank from them both and curled up against the pillows. She panted and glared with rage at something just in front of her on the bed. There was nothing there. They all stood amazed and paralyzed, bewildered by her intensity. She gripped the quilt in her fists and leaned forward as if she meant to attack. Her voice was unearthly when she shrieked:

"Leave him alone!"

. . . and the vampire started awake and pulled away from the neck of the man beneath him. What was the sound that had just commanded him? In all the hundreds of years he'd spent wandering through the relentless night, he'd never heard a command before. He'd been lying here in a swoon all night, his fangs at rest in the jugular. He'd drunk his fill, and he liked to wait till the crack of dawn before he finished a victim off. Thus did he flirt with his own death. The taste of the blood at the end of the night was a thousand times more rapturous. He would float down into his tomb, and his sleep would swarm with kingdoms.

But who was that who called to him? He heaved himself away from Jonathan's body and went to the window to listen. The pitch of the night had lightened into gray, and there was nothing there in all the miles of silence he looked out on. He longed to follow the call, as if the tone of command he'd heard had sounded like a declaration of love. But he had no time. He turned from the window and looked with utter indifference at the body on the bed, though pints and pints of blood still waited to be drawn, he'd had enough for now. The fangs withdrew up under the fishlike lip. The rest would keep for another day.

He swept his cloaks about him and wandered out, a longing beginning to grip him deeper than blood. He groped for the words that had reached him across the darkened plains. If he'd only been capable of an act of goodness, he would have done it now, in homage to her. But all he had to give her was the thronging of his fatal power, and he burned with a fury to lay the world to waste to reach her. In his hand, the whole night long, he had clutched the pendant like a talisman. The pin had dug itself into his bloodless palm, and it held secure as he flew through tunnel and dungeon, down to his ancient grave. And now he knew that, even more than he wanted to kill the world, he wanted that voice to call and call till he came to claim it. He had found his queen at last.

At the end of the scream, Lucy sank back against the pillows, and the doctor chafed her wrists and called her name. He could feel the feverish heat in her skin begin to abate. The speed of the pulse was slowing. As the first ray of the sun shot through the window, she woke as if from a soundless sleep. She looked up at Doctor van Helsing in some surprise, then at the others, and then she took it in that she'd come somehow to Schrader's house.

"How did I get here?" she asked, and though she could see that none of them knew, she was sure that the force of darkness had begun to make its move.

"You've had a bout of fever, Lucy," the doctor said. "I think you'd better stay with Mina, for a few days anyway, till you regain your strength."

They all stood about her bed solicitously. She was going to have the best of care. Rest was what she needed. She only had to ask, and they'd get her whatever she wished.

But they must have sensed the power of her resolve, because one by one they looked down at the floor in a kind of shame, and then they withdrew from the room. They knew they had to let her go. And she rose from the bed and threw off the robe and went to Mina's cupboard. She found enough clothes to get her home. If the fever had burned in her still, till she fainted at every step, still she would have gone. They had come to the eve of the battle, and she had to be alone to think.

When she came downstairs, they stood about as if they'd lost their voices. She could tell they'd be glad to see her go, so they could get on with the frail business of the day-to-day. She didn't even blame them. But she stopped as she passed the doctor, who sat in Mina's parlor, brooding over his roll and coffee.

"Doctor," she said, "I'm going to drop by and return your books. There are some things I have to talk over with you."

"Whenever you wish," he replied.

And she went through the streets and watched the town wake up. The pity welled up in her. Was it better, she wondered, that they didn't know? Was it a kind of mercy that let them go on about their business till the end? She didn't know what she believed in anymore, beyond herself. She didn't try to see beyond the devastation, to when the battle was done. She did not suppose she would live so long. She went through the dappled streets, waving at all her neighbors, and knew she was going to have to give herself completely if anyone else were going to survive. The thought of it filled her with calm.

The sun rose over the wooded hill and flashed on the stones of Dracula's castle. The towers seemed to shrink and writhe at the thought of another day, but power yielded to power, and the balance was struck again. In the bay-windowed room high above the dead garden, Jonathan Harker opened his eyes. He was swept with a wave of nausea as he reached a hand to the pain in his neck. It was swollen up as fat as an apple, so he couldn't talk and could scarcely swallow. He felt so weak he thought he would faint before he was quite awake. But his memory didn't fail him, and his eyes widened with horror as he relived the black of the night.

He struggled up. He gathered his things from about the room and crammed them into his pack. But he seemed to realize there was nothing there he cared about. He knew the vampire had robbed him of his most prized possession, though he couldn't just now recall what it was. But he didn't let the lapse of memory make him panic. He had only to get away, he knew, and things would begin to come back again. He left the sum of his puny worldly goods on the bed and rushed from the room without a backward look. It fortified him, somehow, cleared his head of the pain and dizziness, not to be encumbered by his things.

He wandered the dark passageway, all around the castle, but as before, he found every door locked. His rage and determination mounted. When he reached the dining hall, he saw that the rats were swarming over the table, fighting over the food. He didn't care, and he didn't shrink away. He strode to the fireplace and grabbed the iron fire-rake hanging at the chimney. He went to the door by which he'd first entered and hacked at the lock till it sprang.

But he must have gotten turned around, because it only led to a set of stairs that curled down into the darkness. He was caught in a maze, but he knew he could only go blindly forward, till the castle understood he wouldn't be deterred. At the bottom of the stairs he entered into a long subterranean hall. The walls were moist and cold, and the stench of fungus made him choke. But far away he discerned a glow of light, and he went toward it.

At the end of the hall, a domed room broadened out in front of him, lit by a ring of candles glimmering from the walls. In the center of the space was a great stone dais, on top of it a sarcophagus hollowed out for a king. It was carved all around with glyphs and cursive writing, and the stone lid bore a relief of a pack of wolves tearing a man to pieces. Jonathan went toward it fearlessly. It was almost as if he dared to violate the vampire as the vampire had violated him. He heaved at the stone lid, and it gave a couple of inches. An unspeakable smell of offal rose from the unblessed earth like the coupling of sin and death. But he grunted and pushed again as if the realm of day had triumphed. He was obsessed with the need for final proof, to behold it as no man ever had before. The lid fell over and crashed, stone against stone.

And Dracula lay in state, his cape around him like a pair of wings. He was utterly still, and time was stopped. He stared out of open eyes at the endless waste of his kingdom. Nothing so final as death had stopped his yearning. The core of all evil was concentrated here, and the waiting had only made it more profound. Jonathan felt the word rise out of his throat like the rattle out of a corpse: *Nosferatu!*

But he knew just what to do. He staggered away and groped along the hallway. He had only to make his way to his room again and fashion a stake. And then he would come and drive it into the vampire's heart. *Nosferatu, Nosferatu,* he repeated over and over, running down the hall. He had faced the horror on its own ground, and now he had the power to end it. Before the day was out, it would go back to being what it always was—just a bad dream. The hallway, the stairs went on and on, but Jonathan's faith grew stronger with every step. He saw himself trailing back down the mountain, his strength returning as of old. By the time he reached the streets of Wismar, he would be a proper gentleman again. And he and Lucy would only love each other more for the terror that had stood for the briefest time between them. Everything would be just as before, except more so.

And when at last he stumbled up the stairs and came out into the dining room, he felt a majesty spark his every stride. He came to the table and swept a tangle of rats away. He picked up his knife and went to the ancient chest to hack away a length of wood. No time to return to his room.

No time at all.

The clock began to chime behind him. He turned with an unbelieving gasp. The day could not have fled away again. It was only moments ago that he'd woken to the dawning light in his window. The knife still in his hand, he fled the chiming clock and raced through the tunnel to his room. He could hear the twelfth chime sound as he threw the door back. The room was dim with moonlight.

He let out a cry of rage and ran to the window to challenge the night, but the sight in the courtyard below strangled the words. The vampire's black-veiled horses stood at attention in front of a cart piled high with a pyramid of coffins. The vampire dragged a coffin up the steps from the devastated garden. Pulling it onto his back, he climbed up into the back of the cart and heaved it on the pile. He came around to the front and jumped up into the seat. The horses began to move, and the vampire turned up his face as if to speak to the lonely sky. But he gazed at Jonathan with an air of triumph. He held the reins in one of his long, unspeakable hands, and he slipped the other into his cape. As the horses passed through an arch and out of the courtyard—soundless, soundless—he brought out the pendant. It shone when the moonlight blinked against it. But he could not click it open, because the vision inside it belonged to him.

The cart was gone, and Jonathan knew it would not stop till it crossed the canal at High Street and rolled along into Wismar. Jonathan roared like an animal. He pulled the curtains off the windows. He turned to the bed, tore the linen away, and sat on the floor to rip it into strips. Though he worked for half an hour to make a rope to free himself. He growled and panted

75

like a rabid dog ,all the while he worked. It was as if he'd given up the title to his civilized state and yielded to the savage irrevocably. What good would it do this man to make it back to Wismar? How would he sit and listen to sonatas? How say a word of flattery at dinner?

Perhaps it was only a trick of the eye, in a land too long given over to the moon and the wolves. Perhaps it was really a nobleman's rage, a tragic hero's passion, that had him cursing and tearing his sheets. He hurled the patchwork linen rope from the high bay window. He tied the end to the post between the casements. He flung himself over the side like a dancer, and a gymnast's grace was in his muscled arms as he hurtled down. When the knot at the top snapped, and he fell like a stone the last ten feet, the cry he gave was neither mad nor animal. It quivered with pain like a widow's cry.

He came down on the cobbled court in a heap. He moaned as he turned on his side and went into a crouch. He'd twisted a leg. His shoulder burned with a dislocated bone. But he had to move, and he made as if to stand. He fell on his face, so the gypsy boy, when he came around the archway, must have thought he had fallen dead. Jonathan heard the fiddle strike up. He struggled to swim out of the swoon, to beg for help. But the song had caught him up, and in a moment he was wandering down a lane of chestnut trees, where not a leaf had fallen.

The day was chaotic with storms in the river valley. The river had swollen in the night, and it burst its banks and drowned the summer trees. It made its way out of the mountains with a gathering urgency, hurrying its dark cargo to the sea. A raft of forest trees came drifting down. A pyramid of coffins rose from its surface like a kind of temple. Three old oarsmen stroked at the corners. The money in their pockets was enough to make them princes when they reached the harbor town, and the haunted look in their eyes told what they paid in exchange. Everything went forward irreversibly. As the raft swept past the forests, the leaves began to turn. The animals flocked away downstream, desperate to flee. The hunters roaming the woods by the shore put their guns to their heads. The fishermen standing hip-deep in the stream, a line along the current, pitched themselves in and drowned when the raft went by. Nothing was the same. Nothing could ignore it. And death was the kindest thing it brought.

A day's ride out from Dracula's castle, where the mountain peaks were not so jagged and the flowers and birds began again, lay a nunnery built to the glory of God that had held its summit since deep in the Middle Ages. The cornerstone was laid, the peasants believed, in the very year that the first wall rose at the castle. The mountain folk further believed they were descended from the builders of one or the other. And when a life was dark and full of violence and demons, they said his ancestor set the stones of Dracula's kingdom. When a life would prosper, blessed with love and many children, he would thank his stars that his father's father, a hundred generations back, had worked for a beggar's wages to build the nuns their mountain sanctuary.

The Mother Superior brought the doctor through the quiet halls to a simple room fitted out as a kind of hospital with scrubbed wood floors and a row of perhaps a dozen beds. Two sisters hovered about the prone and restless figure of Jonathan. One dipped a cool cloth in a basin of water and applied it to his forehead. The gypsies had brought this man to the nunnery's door, propped up in a wagon. They delivered their burden gently, carrying him unconscious to the bed where he now lay, but they wouldn't answer the sisters' questions. No one knew where he had fallen or who he was. Though he'd woken at last, he was still delirious.

The doctor sat by the bed and swathed the injured shoulder with bandages. He attended to the swelling in the leg with a cold compress. And he tried not to listen to the wild despair that rose like a chant from the fevered state.

"Coffins, coffins," Jonathan repeated over and over. "We cannot stop the coffins. The sky is silent. The kingdom of plagues is upon us."

He tried to rise from the bed, and the doctor pressed him back into the pillows. Again Jonathan slipped beneath the surface and went unconscious. The doctor packed his bag and went away with the Mother Superior, recommending rest and simple food. They had heard the delirious cries of wounded men for years and years, and they'd learned to turn a deaf ear. But the two nuns in Jonathan's room were scared. They knelt by his bed and prayed and waited for him to speak again, as if he were a prophet.

The river met the sea at Varna, widening through the coastal plain till it loosed itself in the harbor mouth. The bustling piers were lined with ships at anchor, and the city was proud of the commerce it did with the four corners of the earth. Varna's ships came in laden with precious goods, and they went out heavy with lumber and ore from the mountains. The customs officials went from pier to pier, keeping lists and tallies, issuing permits. Nothing was out of place, and nothing ever went wrong. The industry of men and ships went forging ahead at full throttle. Everyone had more money than he knew what to do with.

The *Demeter* was docked at Pier Nine, making ready for a journey down the coast. The dock laborers dragged heavy bags of grain across to the scales to be weighed, then up the swaying gangplank. They had loaded nearly everything by now but the pyramid of coffins waiting mutely, stacked outside the harbormaster's office.

The customs lieutenant, when he arrived, summoned Captain Krull from the deck of the *Demeter*. He barely glanced at the rest of the cargo, but he demanded to see the papers for the coffins, as if someone were playing a joke on Varna's serious business.

"Garden soil," said the captain flatly. "For botanical experiments. One way from Varna to Wismar." He had already had to explain it to his crew, two of whom were so superstitious that they'd signed off and gone out drinking. He'd had to hire replacements when he already had a thousand things to do to keep to his schedule. He wished he'd never said yes to the grizzled oarsmen who'd floated up to his ship at anchor in the middle of the night. But then, there were sums of money a man could not say no to.

"I want to make sure," the lieutenant announced officiously, though the papers were all in order. "I'll have to have one of them opened. That one," he said, pointing arbitrarily into the pile.

The captain cursed, but he called his second mate over, and they wrestled the coffin out of the pile. The mate took a crowbar and prised it open. The soil inside was so black it must have come from a mile deep in the earth. But as the bill of lading said, it was only soil. "Empty it out!" the lieutenant ordered, still unsatisfied. He didn't have a clue to what he was looking for, but he couldn't let the matter go. So the captain and mate overturned the coffin and spilled the earth on the dock. The lieutenant grabbed up the crowbar and poked it about, but there was nothing out of the ordinary.

While the mate was left to clean up, the captain and the lieutenant went across to the harbormaster's office, to sign a sheaf of permits. The mate went off to the laborers' shed to get a spade. And when it was quiet, the pile of earth on the dock erupted, and twenty rats scurried out. They had already found their hiding places by the time the mate returned. He shoveled the soil back into the coffin, and, just as he was done, a rat ran across his foot. He leapt back angrily. He'd always heard the coast was cleared of rats. Which went to prove you couldn't believe the things you heard, he thought as he bent down and clutched his ankle. The hungry little creature had nipped him. He rubbed a bit of spit along the tender spot. It was nothing. Two tiny punctures in the skin, no more than if a pair of gnats had bitten both at once.

Doctor van Helsing sat in his solid office. As director of the hospital, he commanded the corner office above the harbor square, and he spent as much time staring out to sea as he did with his records and experiments. He considered himself a philosopher as well as a technician. He thought long and hard about the meaning of illness. He had come to believe that a good deal of what he treated began and ended in the head. He hated superstition. As a man of the modern world, he was a skeptic in religious matters, Christian or otherwise. But he kept the lion's share of his opinions to himself.

In front of him on the desk were a microscope and a row of test tubes. The bookshelves were crowded with thick volumes, the latest findings in the literature. Everywhere about the walls hung anatomical charts, but the one directly in front of him, which he seemed to ponder as patiently as he did the sea, was a map of the human brain. He was looking at it now, his hand grasped around a formaldehyde jar. In the jar was a newborn suckling, crouched in the fetal position, the head opaque and deformed. Whoever was knocking at the door had to knock several times to break his reverie.

"What is it?" he asked impatiently, and his heart sank when the door opened, admitting the warden from the lunatic ward. The warden and the doctor disagreed at the philosophical level. The warden considered himself a jailer, and the prisoners were his private freakshow.

"We got a real prince brought in," he announced with an icy smile. "He had a fit in the market square. Went over a fence and jumped a sheep. Bit it clean through the jugular."

"Where is he now?"

"Solitary," the warden said. "I had to rough him up a bit. To quiet him down."

The two men hurried through the whitewashed corridors, down the spiral stairs to the low-lit unit where the mad were kept. Doctor van Helsing had to fight the town council, the directory board, his staff and nurses even, for every penny he spent down here. He argued that these unfortunates spoke a secret language that held the key to all men's sorrows. Research on the twisted process of their minds, he felt, was the wave of the future in finding whole new forms of healing. But the mad were a terrible sort of rebuke to Wismar. Privately, most men wished them dead.

Doctor van Helsing gasped when he saw the name chalked on the barred door of the patient's cell: RENFIELD. Too much trouble befalling the Harkers, he thought as the warden unbolted the door. The narrow cell was empty except for a wooden bedstead nailed to the floor. The patient was curled on the bed like an animal, stark naked. He hid his face in his arms and made a sucking sound. The doctor felt a pang of despair, as he always did, as if a madman had ducked behind a curtain, impossible to follow. He went to the bed and laid a comforting hand on Renfield's shoulder.

Renfield's face was like a goblin's when he turned. The tongue jabbed out of his mouth, and his eyes rolled. He tore his hair. He scampered off the bed and flung his hand out into the air and brought it to his mouth. The doctor tried to study the motion, to decipher it like a dance.

"What he's doing," the warden said with a sneer, "is catching flies. That's what he eats."

But Renfield foamed at the mouth with sorrow, because he'd eaten up all the flies and spiders, the moths and fleas in his cell. He caught at the air and came up empty-handed. Then he began to grunt, the one word repeated again and again. "Blood, blood, blood," he moaned. He dropped to a crouch on the floor, clutching his knees in anguish. A pool of urine spread out beneath him on the floor.

"He's a bloody animal, that's what he is," said the warden, and he kicked the groaning man in the spine and sent him sprawling.

"Stop it, stop it," cried the doctor, stepping between them. He pulled the warden away toward the door, anguished to think he could find no better than this vile man to keep the asylum. He wondered if Lucy's wish to speak with him had anything to do with Renfield's breakdown. "I am going to get him some opium," he said. "You stay here till I return. He might hurt himself. And if I see you abuse him again, I'll call in a constable."

The doctor went, and the warden chuckled at his idle threats. He took a pouch of tobacco from his vest. He held a paper between his fingers and tapped a bit of tobacco inside. He wasn't paying a bit of attention. And Renfield rose from the floor, a ghastly grin on his face, and tiptoed forward slowly, soundless as the vampire's horses. With a cry of power, he leapt on the warden's shoulders and brought him to the ground. The wind went out of the warden, and he groveled. Renfield clawed at his face. With a terrifying force, he drove a finger into the warden's eye and gouged it out.

And then the madness rang in the cell like tigers. The warden shrieking, a hand at his bloody face, and

Renfield howling half like a clown, half like a wolf. The guards came running. They handed the warden out to the surgeon, then backed Renfield laughing into the corner. They beat him about the head as they wrapped him into a straitjacket. They threw him down on the wooden bed as if they would break his bones. But he didn't seem to feel a thing, and he looked up smiling, a light in his eyes like a martyr. And he said:

"Can you hear it? The sails are rustling, and the wind is high. The Master comes to release us."

Captain Krull had never seen such a storm on the coastal route. He had to make his way to the open sea to ride it out, and he lost two days. But the *Demeter* was not in any danger. The sea exulted about its bow and bore it aloft like a plundered treasure. The gray waves seethed at the gray sky above, as if the two would come together at last. The captain stood on the bridge and watched the sea surrender its rhythm, as if it would never go back again to tides and seasons. He couldn't shake the feeling that he was to blame.

He sat in his cabin among his maps and instruments, trying to think it out. He opened the log to enter what details he could, but the lurch and roll of the ship turned all he wrote to a tangled scribble. He avoided the thirty men under his command, fearful that one or another might point an accusing finger at him. He brooded and lost track of time, letting the first mate take command of securing the ship. Sometimes he almost wished they would go under and be done with it, yet he seemed to understand they were charmed, doomed to make it through to the other side.

The mate came in to report, wet to the skin and haggard. "Second mate," he said, "is down with fever, Captain." And Krull stood up to follow, knowing that all command had passed to a higher power.

The two men made their way belowdecks, to the crew's quarters next to the hold. In the dim light of a single lantern, a line of hammocks swayed in the motion of the heavy seas. In one of them lay the delirious sailor, his face all ghastly with fear and pain. "He's been raving all morning," the mate said flatly. "He says it's something here on board that made him sick." And he stood at attention while the captain bent to comfort the man in the hammock.

"Sailor," the captain whispered, "you're going to have to ride it out. We'll be in Wismar in a day or two, as soon as the storm breaks. Then we'll get you a doctor, and he'll fix you up good as new."

The second mate breathed with a rattle. Pearls of sweat gleamed on his forehead. One side of his neck was swollen up to the size of an apple. And he looked through a haze of incoherence, focusing with effort on the captain's face. Krull could see the pity in his eyes.

"Oh, Captain," he moaned, "you will curse the day you went to sea, just as I do now. Your ship is a fountain of death. It will not spare a living soul."

"Please," the captain said, trying to calm him. "You are only having visions. It is the fever talking."

And the sick man rolled with a hideous sort of laughter choking in his throat. He raised one bony hand and pointed a shaking finger into the darkness. "Look on the vision I have wrought," he gasped, and Krull followed the gesture, peering into the shadows. Through a net of ropes and a litter of lashed-down barrels, he saw the pile of coffins glimmering in the hold. The rattled laughter went on and on, and he thought his heart would break.

Lucy was packing up her books, checking her notes and marking places here and there, when Mina came to tell her the news of Renfield's fit in the market square. Lucy had planned to visit Doctor van Helsing and talk out her theory of premonitions, her dread of the evil she knew was close upon them, but word of

Renfield's madness made her falter. She slumped into a chair. There wasn't any hope. She would end up crazed herself, and the warden's men would cart her off to a barred cell in the asylum. How could she go to van Helsing now? Would he not call the guards himself?

Mina sat on the window seat and took her hand. She was full of a proud and willful self-assurance that was motivated, she felt sure, by compassion for Lucy's distress. She knew precisely what the problem was, and it was time for her to speak.

"I know just what you're feeling, Lucy," she said. "No letter again. How often must we tell you? Getting mail across the Carpathians is very, very difficult. We have heard besides that the region is pelted with storms. But to be so full of worry is not proper. How can you think it will help poor Jonathan?"

"Jonathan?" She turned her attention to Mina at last. "Oh, something terrible has happened to him, of that I have no doubt. I need no letters. His name is written on the air in letters of fire. Yet if I knew where he was right now, I would set out and not stop walking till I touched his hand."

"You are morbid and unseemly," scolded her sister-in-law. "There is no need for all this drama. Everything will be fine. The Lord will hear our prayers, as He always has."

"The Lord?" she asked, as if she could not place the name. She drew her hand away from Mina and stood and stared out onto the canal. "The Lord is so far from us now, He cannot hear a word. The sound of the whirlwind drowns us out. But I think I do not blame Him. He has had to bear so much evil. I think He is quite as alone as we are now."

"No!" Mina cried. "It is all *you*!" She raised her hand and grabbed at Lucy's hair, pulling away the black ribbon. The hair tumbled down on Lucy's shoulders. "You curse the rest of us for the grief you've caused yourself. You *drove* your husband out of Wismar! He fled in shame because his wife talked like a witch!"

"Mina," Lucy said, her voice as calm and resigned as ever, "there is not much time. You must look to yourself and see how frail the world is all around us. No false hope. The night is coming, and we must walk naked."

"No!" she cried again, holding her hands against her ears. "You have consorted with the devil, and now you try to soil those whom you envy. You hate us for being perfect. You always have. But you'll see how we rid ourselves of vileness." And on that note of triumph, she fled the room and ran from Lucy's house.

She had to *tell* someone. If they didn't chase Lucy out of Wismar, her omens and corruption would set in like rot. So Mina ran through the streets, her anger whipped to a frenzy, and beat on the door of the town council. But they were all at lunch. She ran to the house of the mayor, and no one came to answer the bell. The mayor was back in his garden, his hand in the housemaid's blouse. Mina raged through Wismar, trying to find an official powerful enough to pass the judgment. She came in the end, weary and unsatisfied, to the door of the bishop's church.

With a righteous air, she walked on in. She knew what it meant to be chosen, and she came here full of a certainty of a higher and higher election. She loved this place for its decorousness—the candles and flowers, the silver vessels and handworked linen. She drifted up the aisle serenely, like a kind of priest herself. She knew her God was with the laws and not the prophets.

But when she reached the altar, she saw in the glow of its flickering lights that rats had tipped the wine and mauled the bread. They swarmed at the base of the cross, gnawing on one another's limbs. And there wasn't a sound in all their scrambling. Not a sound in the whole high temple but the sound of Mina's scream.

A commotion broke out in the sickroom at the nunnery. Jonathan stood up on swaying legs and went to the cabinet to retrieve his clothes. The sisters pleaded and tried to lead him back, but he shook them off as if he were desperate. He tore off his nightshirt and stood there naked in front of them, and they ran from the room to summon the Mother Superior.

By the time she'd arrived, he had dressed himself in breeches and shirt, and he sat on the edge of the bed to draw on his heavy, gray woolen socks. He grunted at the pain in his shoulder. Though his leg had healed enough for him to hobble around, his head was pounding still with the shock of his accident. He didn't look as if he would make it a mile before he collapsed.

"You'll hurt yourself worse," the Mother warned him from the doorway. "Then you'll have to start all over."

"I am Jonathan Harker, and I live in Wismar," he said with a bitter irony. "That is all I know. If I don't go home and find out what has exiled me, I will kill myself with grieving."

"But you didn't remember so much as *that* till only yesterday. The rest will come back. What is so urgent?"

"I don't *know*," he cried. "But I see this train of coffins bearing down on Wismar, and I have to go and warn them. Mother, why will you not tell me what you know of the castle where I spent three days that have left my mind a blank?"

They faced each other across the room. He stood up and held the bedpost and looked at her accusingly. She wrung her hands. She had lived here fifty years, had heard every superstition in the neighborhood, but still, after all this time, could hardly put the matter into words.

"We pray against the darkness, Mr. Harker. The darkness is all about us, of course, but we try not to inquire too deeply into it. We find that we do more good when we turn our faces to the light. No doubt it is most old-fashioned of us, but that is how it has been handed down for us to do."

But he hardly listened. He cupped his hands and stared into them—searching, searching—as if he meant to read his fortune off his palm. It was the way he held the pendant when he gazed on Lucy's portrait. He remembered none of that, of course, but he felt an echo of something, even so. As if there were someone still in Wismar who knew who Jonathan Harker was. And he was willing to bet on that small hope, because he couldn't endure the sense of doom and the feeling that he was only letting it happen if he stayed here.

"I have no money," he said, pulling on first one boot, then the other. "I will make it up to you one day, I promise."

"I cannot convince you to stay just a few more days? Till you've grown a little stronger?"

"No," he replied quite firmly, but he came across the room and took her hands. "May I ask you to pray for me?"

"You do not have to ask," the old woman said, taking his arm so they walked together along the loggia and onto the porch. "And I will tell you a curious thing. Whatever evil was there in the castle has gone. I know it when I pray. There has always been a kind of fury in the air." And she swept her free hand vaguely around her head. "No more. And though it ought to make me weep for joy, I find I am growing terrified."

"What is it?" he pleaded.

"I wish I knew. But as long as I cannot convince you to stay and rest, then let me urge you to hurry home. I fear there is not much time. As you are

Count DRACULA (Klaus KINSKI) in his crypt.

A tender moment on the beach for Jonathan (Bruno GANZ)
and Lucy (Isabelle ADJANI).

Count DRACULA (Klaus KINSKI) pours wine for Jonathan (Bruno GANZ) at their first supper after his arrival at the castle.

The coach returning the gravely ill Jonathan HARKER back to Wismar.

Lucy (Isabelle ADJANI) awakens from a nightmare.
The vampire (Klaus KINSKI) enters Lucy's (Isabelle ADJANI) bedroom.

Vampire (Klaus KINSKI) and victim (Isabelle ADJANI).
The vampire (Klaus KINSKI) greedily sucks blood from
Lucy (Isabelle ADJANI).

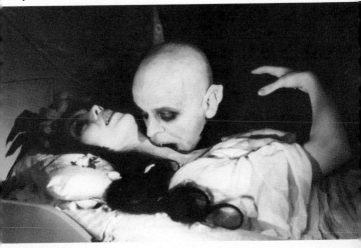

Plague-infested rodents spill off the *Contamarra* into Wismar.

A procession of coffins containing plague victims.

Lucy (Isabelle **ADJANI**) sprinkles the crumbs of a conse-crated host over the vampire's hideaway coffin to keep him from reentering.

The first rays of sun destroy the vampire (Klaus **KINSKI**).

skeptical of prayer, please take this gift from us to speed you on your way."

And he followed her pointing finger down the tree-lined courtyard, to where a russet horse, saddled and ready to ride, was tied to a hitching post. She'd been hoping he'd go along, he realized. He bowed low and walked away at a brisk pace. Though he winced at the pain in his shoulder, he had a momentary sense that all would be well. The world was a reasonable place, and a man who determined to find out who he was was bound to succeed beyond his wildest dreams. He mounted like a general, turned to wave, and trotted out the gate with a gathering sense of mission. The Mother Superior sketched a blessing in the air. She stood on the nunnery porch and watched him go down the mountain path, staring into the distance long after he was out of sight.

Five

THE sea was still gray and violent, but the storm had withdrawn enough for the *Demeter* to set sail. On the icy deck, under a pewter sky, the captain and his mate lashed a plain wooden cross to a shrouded corpse. They stood at the rail, sleepless and numb, and tried to pray for the soul of their brother seaman. But they had already buried twenty men at sea in five days' time, and the words they used to call on God began to seem like a mockery. "Mercy on his soul," the captain mumbled, and they picked up the corpse and heaved it overboard. Dully, they watched it hit the water, float for a moment in their wake, and sink.

"How many are we now?" the captain asked.

"Six," the other replied. But they both knew the four sailors still alive were already sick with the fever. They lay in their hammocks in the stinking space belowdecks, where the air had turned rotten like a charnel house. "I implore you, Captain," he said, his voice near breaking, "we must turn back. Or at least seek shelter in the nearest port."

"Out of the question," replied the captain fervently.

"I will carry my principles with me to the bottom, if I have to, but I will not abandon the voyage. We go on for the sake of those poor men who have aleady died. Man prevails. There is no other law."

And so saying, he staggered to his cabin while the mate went up to the bridge to take the wheel. Krull could hear the moaning of the fevered sailors down below as he sat at his desk and turned the page of the *Demeter*'s log. He entered the name of the man just buried as if he were keeping the book of the dead, preparing for a judgment day that was drawing ever nearer.

"We are true to our course," he wrote in a trembling hand. "Northwest at thirty degrees. Wind is steady. Twelve knots."

He had run this ship for eighteen years. He had traveled overland to the North Sea shipyard where she was built, to watch her fitted. There were three or four men, the first mate included, who'd been with him since the day the *Demeter* left port on its first coastal run. He was a man who understood the gamble he made with fate every time he put to sea. But though he could accept storms and shoals, running aground and whirlpool as part of the lot of a captain's life, he couldn't face the thought that his ship was being broken up from within. He had to force himself to record the ominous details.

"We are burdened with a curse, it seems. Twenty men lost to fever, and four vanished without a trace. The rumor circulates among the men—it comes on them when the fever reaches its crisis—that there is some stranger aboard. We search from stem to stern, but there is nothing there. Nothing but rats. The *Demeter* has never been so overrun."

He put aside his quill and held his head in his hands. He knew what the cruelest twist of fate would be. He was going to be the last survivor. Racked with guilt and shame, he dashed across his cabin to the ship's safe. He twirled the dial through the set of the combination. He creaked the door open, thrust his hand inside and came out with the roll of bills the oarsmen had paid him. Groaning with sorrow, he tore at it till it shredded. He staggered to the porthole above his desk and threw the money out onto the waves.

The sea was not interested in being paid. No amount of money was enough. But he turned from the gesture with a renewed sense of command, and he walked across to the door, ready to take the wheel of his beloved ship. He had to hold on to the wall at every second step, but he made his slow way up the deck. He didn't even seem to realize that the fever had come upon him.

Lucy was subdued when the nurse ushered her into the doctor's office. Van Hesling stood up eagerly at his desk and came around to embrace her, but the somber mood stayed his hands at the last moment. He waited for her to speak first. She put down her stack of books on the edge of the desk, looked blankly at the fetal pig in the jar, and slowly took off her gloves. She was wearing a dress that was gray and very severe, and her wide-brimmed hat was plain as a Quaker's. She was no less beautiful than before—more, perhaps, with the procelain glow that had come to her white, white skin—but still it was a shock to see her so. In the past she had always favored colors bright as a garden.

"I have come to ask a favor," she said.

"Of course, dear Lucy," the old man said, bringing up a chair for her. "You mentioned you had some things you wanted to discuss. Something's come up in your reading, perhaps." He tapped the topmost book as he sat at the desk.

"Oh, no," she said, shaking her head and looking away. "Not yet. You wouldn't believe me." She stated it as a matter of fact, without any rancor or accusation. "What I need to do—I have to talk to Renfield."

"Impossible!" exclaimed the doctor, leaning forward. "He wouldn't even know you, Lucy. You can do nothing to help him, good as you are. I must insist that you turn your mind to more cheerful matters. Wismar sorely misses your gaiety, you know."

"I think he will talk to me," she insisted. "I know he cares for me greatly, and besides, we share a common . . . vision, if you will. He is the only one who can ease my mind about Jonathan. Will you have me go mad myself with worry?"

He couldn't say no to Lucy. He looked at her longingly for a moment, as if he could bring them both back to the simpler time when she was a child who ran to him laughing, whenever he came to call. It touched him that Lucy was not afraid of the mad like the others. Renfield had so far ceased to be violent that they had taken him out of the straitjacket. Van Helsing believed that a generous soul like Lucy could have the most salubrious effect. He had only said the contrary in order to protect her. But he saw again how strong she was, and he felt new hope himself as he beckoned her to follow.

"There is the most extraordinary swing in his behavior," he explained as they walked downstairs and past the guards. "At times he is so lucid I feel like bringing him up to my office to talk. For the rest, he is in a kind of trance. But what is most curious, he never seems to experience melancholy or anguish. Not since the first day. He seems to be in such a state of peace."

A guard unbarred the door, and they entered the cell. Renfield sat cross-legged on the wooden bed, his head turned dreamily up toward the high barred window. He couldn't climb up to see out of it, but the patch of sky he saw from where he sat seemed quite sufficient. He was stark naked. One hand played with his genitals. Van Helsing was so captivated by the madman's mood that he neglected to apologize for any offense the lady might have taken. But the lady hardly noticed.

"Mr. Renfield," she sad, "I don't know what I shall do. I haven't had word from Jonathan in weeks. If only I knew the name of the place where you sent him. . . ."

"Jonathan Harker of Wismar. Is that the man you speak of?" the madman asked. His voice was very tender—sleepy, almost, except his eyes were round and wide. He stared at her just off center. He seemed to revere the name, as if his house agent had gone away to war and acquitted himself like a hero.

"You've had word of him?" Lucy demanded, coming close and sitting by him. Not afraid or horrified. She realized now how much time she had lost by running from him eating his butterfly.

"He is a man of noble birth, I believe," said Renfield.

"Not Jonathan," she replied. "You must be thinking of the nobleman he visited. What was *his* name?" She took up his free hand in both of hers, trying to catch his gaze and make him concentrate. "Try to remember, Mr. Renfield. I must get word to my husband."

"He is nothing but a name," the madman said. "He rides like a gypsy, rootless and alone."

"Who? Who do you mean?"

"Half of the man is blood, and half is now a darker thing." Renfield spoke in a singsong, his meaning wrapped in riddles. "Which way will he go? Well, that depends. Fate is not required to flip the coin till later."

"It delights you to tease me, doesn't it?" She rose and walked to the corner, under the window. It was simply amazing, van Helsing thought. She chatted with him as if he were quite as normal as anyone else. Why did everyone always raise their voices and talk to the mad in toneless phrases? She was better at it than he was. "I'm so worried, you know," she went on, "I've half decided to saddle a horse and go myself. I would not cease asking questions till I reached the Carpathian Mountains."

"No, no," cried Renfield, coming up to his knees and putting his hands out pleadingly. "You mustn't do that. He is almost here."

"Do you mean Jonathan Harker?" the doctor demanded.

"The Master," Renfield gasped, as if beatified by the knowledge. "The Master comes at the head of his army. Thirsty, thirsty. Four hundred thousand strong." The last came out in a kind of babble, and the madman lost control. He fell back in a fit, and his mouth foamed over. The bug eyes rolled back into his head, till all they saw was white and blank as grapes.

Doctor van Helsing went over and held Renfield's head, a hand around his jaw so he wouldn't choke on his tongue. Then the doctor looked over to Lucy, thinking to apologize for the madman's losing his grip at the crucial moment. She stood there, cool and impassive, and waited for the fit to subside. Van Helsing realized two things at once. First, she had come to a point where nothing could make her squeamish. She'd assimilated all that was grotesque or festered or coming to pieces. Second, she appeared to know what Renfield was about. The halluncinations were no less real to her than the ordinary chatter.

Renfield quieted down and presently came back to them. The doctor almost forbade her to question further, but he sensed they were on the verge of a breakthrough. It was worth the risk to Renfield's nerves to push him just a little more. And it struck van Helsing again as he gave her the nod to continue

—the sense of Lucy's towering purpose, larger than the stifling cell they sat in now, larger than all of Wismar.

"Army?" she queried, coming close. "Army of what?"

He focused on her slowly as he crouched in the doctor's lap. He grinned in a way that seemed both loving and curiously pure. "*You* know," he said coquettishly. "They fill up your dreams the way they fill up mine. Shall we tell the doctor?"

"Oh please," she said, nodding excitedly.

"It's rats," he announced. "They are white as lambs, and their eyes are full of light. They sweep across the earth like a blanket."

Van Helsing looked from one to the other, and the gravity in their eyes as they locked each other with a stare was so enormous that he shook with terror. He began to think *he* was the one going mad. He pushed Renfield aside and stood up from the bed. Lucy was wide-eyed, but her body seemed limp and impassive as he took her arm and steered her out of the cell. She looked over her shoulder helplessly, holding the eye-to-eye with Renfield, even as she let the doctor take her away. The doctor shut the door. The guard bolted and barred it. Lucy began to weep quietly as they made their way upstairs.

And Renfield sat back in his corner, cross-legged and alone. He looked up again at the square of sky and began to recite. He spoke with a strange officiousness, as if he were a town councillor reading a proclamation in the market square. He had not seen a newspaper since they locked him up. He had spoken with no one from the world at large. He had heard no rumors. Yet his voice was full of the certainty of fact.

"Plague is declared in several places," he intoned. "In Transylvania and the Black Sea port of Varna, an irreversible fever has appeared. Most of those stricken have been young women. All victims have died with puncture wounds at the neck, the origin of which is still unexplained. Whole stretches of land along the coast have withered into dust. The animals throw fits and twitch in the streets. Silence grows and grows."

And in the silence that followed his speech, from out in the hallway there came a muffled cry. The guard had drawn his sword and thrown himself upon it. Blood seeped out and covered the floor like a blanket. As the silence grew, Renfield came off the bed and crawled—soundlessly, soundlessly—to the door. He crouched to the crack of light at the doorsill, put out his tongue in the dust, and waited for the stream to reach him. The room was full of glory.

The horse did all the work. As they came down into a wild and stormy region, Jonathan nodded in the saddle. He held the reins so loosely that he couldn't give directions. For hours at a stretch he slumped forward onto the horse's neck. But the beast seemed to have the will to go on, even when Jonathan didn't, and so they made their way. When the lightning dazzled the air and struck trees down like match-sticks, they sought the shadow of an overhanging rock and waited for the rage to pass. When they came to a stream that tore through the landscape in a torrent, the horse went along it till he found a natural bridge to cross.

Jonathan was too feverish and weak to say how long they'd traveled. They'd left the steepest crags behind long since, and in the meadows on either side of the muddy road began to appear the trees and grasses of the foothills. But it was not till he came through a narrow pass in the gathering dark and decided to stop for the night that he found himself remembering. He came to the middle of the level space, sheltered at last from the driving winds, and saw the remains of a bonfire, many weeks old. *I've been here,* he thought as he dismounted.

He sat by the bed of ashes, arms around his knees, while the horse trailed off to crop the meager grass that grew up among the stones. He remembered a group of people dancing. He looked about him on the empty ground and saw in his mind the gypsy treasure. He could almost hear them whispering behind him, and he strained his ears to recover the words they spoke so long ago. The sound took shape in his head like a shadow on the night: *Nosferatu, Nosferatu.*

His eyes widened in horror. He looked down at the scar on his thumb. He brought his hand up to his neck, where he felt two tiny scabs. He saw the vampire start forward toward him, the night he had slumped against the table, powerless to move. He screamed now as he couldn't then, and the mountains rang around him with the echo. He shuddered at the touch of undead flesh, the heat of the monster's breath against his neck. The whole of the time he was trapped in the castle came back in a flash. The scream went on and on, till he thought the breath would go out of him for good. But at last it was done, and he lay panting in the dirt, his cheek in the muddy ashes. His heart was still again. Then, like a stroke of lightning blazing through his being, he saw to the end of the nightmare. He saw Lucy.

"Lucy," he whispered, as if he'd solved the riddle at last. The face was blazoned on his heart like the portrait on the pendant. The world came back into balance again. For every force of evil, a fire of goodness stood and fought. He knew he would not forget again the anchor of his life. "I am Jonathan Harker of Wismar," he thought to himself with a wild thrill of pride. The terror of the vampire shriveled and died on the spot, like dust among the ashes. He and Lucy together would make the night retreat. He knew he had come to himself again for good.

It was dusk on the open sea. The decks of the *Demeter* were empty of men. The captain stood at the helm, groggy and alone, and every few minutes he seemed to double up with pain. The rats crept over his feet in a trance. They didn't bite, didn't scurry, and didn't search for food. They only waited to reach dry land. The captain hardly noticed them anymore, even when he was lucid. They were as much a part of the journey now as the heavy gray waves of the brooding sea.

But the first mate was still sane enough to feel the horror all about him. He had buried the rest of the men today, heaving them over the side, too tired to sew a shroud around them. He never stopped his search of the ship, but he never knew what he was looking for. Now he stood at the stairway down to the hold, an axe in his hand, and determined to hack his way through all the coffins till he tracked it down. He would sift that black polluted soil between his fingers and hold the secret in his grasp.

He descended into the belly of the ship. He went up fearlessly to the pyramid of coffins. As he heaved the axe and struck at the lid of the nearest one, splintering the wood and letting out a hideous stench on the air, he neglected to notice the shadows building behind the pile. He worked away, and at last he broke open one whole side. He knelt to the hole and pawed at the earth with his hands. He did not know that the sun had set. He was head and shoulders through the hole and into the coffin, digging around in the dirt, when he felt something tugging at the tail of his shirt. He thought it must be the captain, and he pulled out into the gloomy light to say he wouldn't stop till he came to the end of the pile.

He opened his mouth to scream, but the vampire's teeth gripped onto his throat with such a lightning speed that he never made a sound. He was paralyzed in every limb as the vampire shook him by the neck, drinking him in in great gulps. He usually made his incision so precisely, drank the blood at such a heartbeat's rhythm, that his victims died in a kind of swoon. But the vampire raged at the desecration of his temple. He wanted pain. And the mate went out in such an agony that his heart burst in his chest. He was pinned and tortured till he lost his mind, all in the moment that he died.

When every drop was drained, the vampire raced about the room in a sort of drunken madness. He always forgot the awful beauty of violence. The triumph broke in him anew each time. He was swept by a fit of soundless laughter, and he let the blood dry on his fangs, his mouth like an open wound. He pointed a nerveless finger at the corpse, and a wave of rats erupted from the violated coffin, swarmed all over the still-warm flesh, and mangled it with their teeth. Dracula quivered with pleasure as he watched. The drunken delirium passed, and he drew his cape about him and went forward. As he climbed the steps to the main deck, it was clear in his proud demeanor who was in command here.

He went up to the bridge, where the captain fought to stay at the wheel. He came up close and put a hand on Krull's shoulder. The captain didn't flinch—he hardly seemed to notice. They watched the lilt of the evening waves together. They had no one around them anymore to worry about. They kept the ship between them like a secret.

"I thought," said Dracula, "the time had come for us to meet. The cargo you carry belongs to me."

"Yea, though I walk through the valley of the shadow of death, I will fear no evil, for thou art with me," the captain replied. The devil had come to court him. He forced the fever out of his head and turned to the God he had left behind in the harbor town where he was born.

"Nothing is required," said Dracula, "but the courage to be alone. I will need a thousand lieutenants before the month is out. A thousand thousand by the start of winter."

"Thy rod and thy staff they comfort me. Thou preparest a table before me in the presence of mine enemies."

"When it is all over," said Dracula, "I will banish the light of day entirely. We will build beneath the ground tremendous cities. When all the blood is drunk up, there will be no hunger among us."

"I shall dwell in the house of the Lord forever," the captain replied, but the words had turned to ashes in his mouth. They didn't make any sense. He was so weak and weary that he fell against the stranger's icy shoulder. The vampire held him up and put out a free hand to the wheel. When the captain felt the stronger force take over, he turned and buried his face against the stranger's neck. He wept for his loss of strength, for the lies he was taught at the altar rail, for the men he had failed. There was no comfort anywhere but here.

Doctor van Helsing couldn't let the matter go. He had sent Lucy home the moment they came upstairs from Renfield's cell, but the feeling plagued him that the two shared an intuition he had missed. He didn't like to admit it, but it came as a blow to his pride to think that someone other than himself could communicate with a hopeless case. But he genuinely wanted Lucy's thoughts when he rang the bell beneath the chestnut tree that evening.

"Oh," she said when she opened the door. "You're very kind to look in on me, but I'm feeling quite myself again."

They went into the parlor and sat by the fire. The solid oak tables and horsehair sofa, the gaslight glowing from the walls in frosted tulip globes, the mantel clock and the steel engravings—everything in the room anchored them here in the sturdy world of Wismar.

"I was interested in your method with Renfield," he observed. "I wonder if you would consider coming to work with me."

"How many beds have you in the hospital?" she asked abruptly. He sensed that she had not even heard *his* question.

"Sixty."

"Oh, that's not enough. We'll need hundreds. I was wondering if we couldn't set up the school as a sick ward. Or the town hall."

"Lucy, you aren't making sense," he said a trifle harshly. He heaped another spoon of sugar in his coffee.

"It is only a matter of days," she said without any passion. "The plague is coming."

"Don't even *say* it," he gasped, standing up and looking about for his hat. He had heard the rumors of fever at Varna, of course. He wasn't a superstitious man, but he acted as if Lucy had jinxed the town by speaking the word. He seemed very old as he hobbled to the hatrack in the hall.

"It does not matter anymore if you believe me," she said with an odd compassion. "But we might save a good many if we were prepared. We ought to convene the town council. Draw up emergency plans."

"There are no rats in Wismar," the doctor said loudly. "Our streets are clean." And he put on his hat quite crookedly and mumbled his good night. He swung the door wide and padded off into the summer night.

"Please," she called after him, "tell me the moment you know the truth. We mustn't lose hope."

But he had his hands held against his ears, and in another moment he'd crossed the canal and gone out of sight.

Mina opened the cupboard in her kitchen and saw a rat perched on the crust of her pie. She shut the door hard and bustled across the room to pour Schrader's tea. He was sitting at the center table absorbed in his evening paper. He'd already eaten enough dinner for three men, she thought. He didn't need dessert tonight. She put an extra spoonful of honey in his sassafras tea before she set it down in front of him. Then she sat at the table opposite him and folded her hands and tried to stay calm. Behind her husband's head, she could see a rat on the windowsill outside, scratching to come in.

She knew it wasn't really there. They came at her frequently now a couple of dozen a day popping up all over the place, but she knew they were really in her head. And she also understood they were manifestations of sin. Though she went to church and did everything right, she was somehow being punished. She accepted the sentence calmly and struggled to abase herself before the mystery. Whenever Schrader was out of the house, she fell to her knees and prayed. She wore a rough shirt that burned her skin when she moved. When Schrader went to bed, she sat up in the parlor and lit a dozen candles. She read the Bible half the night.

But she didn't dare tell another living soul. Her shame was too great. She knew that the stories of Lucy's perverse behavior had spread to every quarter of the town, and she took a certain pride in keeping her own dark visions to herself. She was sure it was the dividing line between the blessed and the damned. She planned to grope her way to the fount of forgiveness and stand up clean and whole. And she would peer out at Lucy from the gate of heaven and smile in her most beatific way. It was a race for divine election, sinner against sinner, and Mina Schrader willed herself to win.

She spoke the name of God in a fevered prayer,

calling Him to witness her act of worship. *God, God, God,* she thought, chanting in celebration of her victory over sin. She did not know that the word she spoke was not the word she thought. Her voice rang dully in the tidy room, saying it over and over: *Nosferatu, Nosferatu.*

Though the sky was still amass with clouds, a streak of liver-colored light appeared in the eastern sky. The vampire stood at the wheel and cradled the captain like a brother. It was time to turn over the watch, to wake poor Krull from his feverish sleep. The vampire propped him up at the wheel and stooped for a length of rope that was coiled at his feet. Wrapping it round Krull's body, he tied him in a harness so he wouldn't slump over.

"I turn over the daylight command to you," said Dracula, casting his empty eyes on the swooning man. He shook Krull's shoulder vigorously, to wake him, and the captain groaned. His head lolled baring his neck to the vampire's gaze. It was irresistible, of course. Dracula suddenly needed the strength, just to make his way downstairs again, to sink down into his coffin. He bent forward with a predator's instinct and bit down into the vein. He sucked up just enough to fill his mouth. When he withdrew and stood up tall again, a trickle of blood ran down at the corners of his mouth.

Then he seized the captain's shoulders in both his hands. He reeled with intoxication as he shook the man quite violently. Krull woke from a dream of a sunny island harbor where all his noble seamen still survived. Woke to the agony of the claws tearing through his shoulders, the seeping wound in his neck, but when he turned around to cry for mercy, there was no one there. The pressure had lifted on the instant. He looked out sadly on the rising sun, and his nightmare course came back to him. He steered his death ship forward. He had no other choice.

And down in the hold, Dracula creaked back the lid on his coffin. The pendant lay on the earth like a dark flower. He plucked it up and clutched it in his hand as he settled down into his endless bed. The lid closed over him once again. He felt his limbs go rigid. The last of the blood dripped down his throat like a consecrated wine, and he drew back into his cavernous mind. Ever since the night he'd stolen Lucy's portrait, the prospect of spending the livelong day in the tomb had come to seem, if not a welcome thing, then bearable at last. For the first time in several hundred years, he had started to dream again.

They had just come out of the hills. They'd ridden straight down for the last three days like conquering heroes, horse and rider alike. When the straightaway came into view, the horse began to gallop. Jonathan took off his hat and waved it above his head, hurrahing all the while. The slope leveled out, and the road rang like thunder as they galloped, the tall summer fields billowing on either side. He could hear the singing of birds like a chorus of hope.

He hardly had time to notice when the singing stopped. They had covered about ten miles along the plain, bound for the coast and home. Up ahead, an ancient elm soared above a crossroads. A great black bird had waited there, hidden in the midmost branches, for a couple of months or more. It hadn't had anything else to do since the day it delivered the letter to Renfield and Company, one early morning in June. But it seemed to know its time had come. It beat its wings and fell from the branch in a fatal dive. As the horse passed under the tree, the bird swooped in and hit the earth between the galloping legs.

The horse stumbled and his front legs broke when he rocketed forward and fell in the road. Jonathan, thrown to the side, landed in a heap at the field's edge. And though his shoulder roared with the pain again, it seemed he was not meant to die just yet. He was given the harder task of witnessing the vast indifference of fate. He sat up, dizzy and groaning, and looked from one to the other of the ruined creatures in the road. The horse twitched and whinnied, scrabbling at the ground with his two back legs, as if he could run from this bad end. A few feet off, the bird clumped around on its broken neck, its wings like fallen sails.

Jonathan didn't have a gun. He had to use a rock to kill the bird. He cut the horse's throat with his fish knife. Then he sat by the road and wept for the fate of heroes, unable to accept the fact that he'd been stopped by a freak and impossible accident. It was far, far worse. The fate that had a grip on the throat of things didn't waste its time on freak collisions. Everything now, from here on, was part of a master plan. The black bird had always been intended to stop him here if he got this far. All over the world, there were sentinels dark as this in place.

It wasn't fair, he thought bitterly. If he couldn't count on a little luck, perhaps the world didn't deserve to be saved. There was only so much a man could do, and then he had to begin to think about going along with the drift of things. What was he doing anyway, supposing he could save the world? Now all he wanted to do was get back to Lucy and close the door. Let the world tear itself to pieces, if it had to. He and Lucy would go on as before and make a world of their own.

Thus do heroes grow up into practical men. He began to walk along the road, and gradually the calm of the summer day overtook him. He chose not to notice the fields here and there that were withered with blight. A brackish pond where the dead fish floated belly up on the surface. A rain of yellow leaves when he passed under a roadside maple. There was still enough of the summer perfectly grown and blossoming to fill him with humble cheer. I am only Jonathan Harker of Wismar, he thought mildly. Fate was not going to pick him up and toss him down again if *he* had anything to say about it.

When he heard the sound of a coach approaching behind him, he didn't even bother to turn around and flag it down. After all, he didn't have any money. He would have to be content to walk along, maybe fifteen miles a day, till he stopped in a village and worked for his supper. The prospect pleased him mightily, in fact. So he was somewhat taken aback to hear the coachman whoa the horses just ahead of him and lean around in the seat and call him by his Christian name. It was the coachman who'd dropped him off at the fork to Dracula's castle.

"Well, how is the prosperous young estate agent? I bet you've got a fat commission in your pocket, and you're going home to buy yourself a mansion."

"Not exactly," Jonathan said with an easy shrug. "Just now, I am nothing more than a vagabond. I have put away my wild ambitions. I'm making my way back home to live out my life with the beautiful woman I married. That is all I care about right now."

"Admirable!" exclaimed the coachman. "I suppose the least I can do for a man without ambition is offer him passage. Climb in! Wismar is only a little out of the way."

Why did it make him feel so doomed, he wondered as he climbed in. He'd rather hoped to take his time. He was really rather frightened of what might await him at home. He looked out the window, full of dread and confusion. He could see that some of the fields were blighted and brown, and he thought he saw rats running in and out among the broken stalks.

Mina still came every day to fix Lucy's lunch, but a

silence had grown up between them since the day they fought. Lucy wished she could make peace again, but she didn't have time. The mayor had refused to see her again this morning, pleading other business, and the town council was disbanded for its summer recess. She was drawing up her own contingency plans, working out on the map of the city how best to set up quarantine. She marked where the doctors and pharmacists lived. She circled buildings suitable for quick conversion into hospitals. She blocked off a place in every quarter where a last stand could be made, and she sat brooding over her plan like a general when Mina came into the morning room with her lunch on a tray. Mina set the tray down on the table next to the map, then turned to stare out the window at the canal.

"Mina," she said, taking only the tea as she pushed the tray away, "you never give me any news. How are you feeling?"

"Wonderful," Mina replied with an odd fervor. "My blessings overflow my cup."

"How do things seem in Wismar? Do you notice any —changes?"

"I feel a new awakening at hand," she said obscurely. "We are the chosen people, Lucy."

"But tell me, how will it manifest itself?"

"Ah, but the likes of you will not be included, don't you see?" She turned from the window, and Lucy nearly gasped at the fanatic glare that fired her eyes. "Wismar has become a holy place," she said, "and the infidels must be driven from our midst. Every man must strike his enemy down, till the streets have run with blood. Then there will be nothing but angels left in Wismar, and the Lord will take His throne among us."

Like a disembodied wraith, she drifted out of the room and left the house. Lucy sat there numbly for a while. Would they lock Mina up like Renfield, she wondered, or did the veneer of godliness mean she was immune to accusations of insanity? How many walked the streets of Wismar waiting for a prophet? Lucy had long ago gone beyond fear and dread. She endured this latest horror like the others. She moved inexorably forward in her resolve. But she couldn't help but wonder how much more than plague and fever were being loosed upon the land.

The *Demeter* hugged the coastline just to the north of Wismar as the twilight fell. Through the swirl of fog, the captain made out along the beach the corpses of boats gnawed to the bone by wind and sea. The darkness loomed, and he felt that the world lay graveyard to graveyard wherever they passed. Though his hands were roped to the wheel, though he could do nothing but steer to his final harbor at Wismar, he struggled to turn them toward the shore, to break them up among the other carcasses and skeletons. There was only a shred of humanity breathing in him still, but he fought to use it at last to strike a blow against the ravages of evil.

And the shadow fell across him as the vampire came to take the watch. The clawed hand shot out to steady the wheel. With the other, he gripped the captain by the hair and turned his blistered neck to the lunge of the ravening bite. There was so little blood left in the poor racked body that Dracula had to leave off before he had a proper kiss. But he preferred to have it bit by bit to slake his hunger through the night, so he didn't kill quite yet. Krull shivered in his grasp, in an agony of suffering, and Dracula held him close as if the suffering were bliss.

The vampire stood over the sea of rats that covered the deck so deep they had to kill each other to get enough space to breathe. As they drew ever closer to Wismar, the rats began to pant, and the heaving sound reached the ear of the vampire like a song. He held the captain close like a special friend as he addressed the quivering multitude.

"Children of the night," he began, in a voice of gathering majesty, "your ceaseless patience shall end before the next sun rises. Make free with the whole earth. Go retrieve your ancient power, and let it flame. You have waited like a guilty secret in all men's minds, generation upon generation, and now each hour of waiting will be repaid in untold measure. Have leisure in your murdering. The time belongs to us."

And just as he finished his exhortation, he spied the lighthouse at the entrance to the harbor. The glory shot through him so he moaned with delight, and he bent to take another draught. He sucked for a moment, pulled his fangs, and whispered into the captain's ear: "Hold on, my comrade." The rats began to gnash their teeth in expectation. The light high up in the tower seemed to flicker and dim, as if it meant to gutter and hide the entrance. But the wind that had followed them all through the storm puffed the *Demeter*'s sails and waved her past the jetty and in. As they hit the calm of the inner water, the vampire could hear the long scream of the lighthouse keeper, throwing himself from the top of the tower till he dashed on the rocks below.

They passed among the fishing boats of Wismar, and every one seemed to drift away and strain at its anchor, as if trying to flee the death ship's shadow. The vampire was in a frenzy of excitement, feeling how close he was to Lucy, and he kept leaning over to take another gulp of blood, desperate to quiet the passion. By the time they had crossed the harbor and touched the end of the pier, the captain's body was bone dry. Dracula heaved it away from him, so that the captain slumped over the wheel as if he meant to shelter it in death. Dracula leapt from the bridge and ran down the deck to the bow. He stood like a figurehead, arms out like a supplicant. For this one moment,

111

he seemed to doubt the success of his voyage, to doubt the queen he had come to marry for all eternity. He seemed to beseech a higher power, though he was the highest power here.

And then the light of dawn began to show at the edge of the sea, and there wasn't time to assuage his doubt. He had to stagger, nearly out of breath, through the carpet of rats to reach the stairs to the hold. No strength to throw down the plank, so the creatures could run free. No power left in him as he tumbled down the stairs and crawled to the coffins. But in his heart he shrieked revenge against the dawning day. Before another night had passed, he vowed as he crept back into the earth, he would lie in state in his own land. When he went down into the tomb again, he would sleep with an angel wrapped in his cloak. And his multitude of rabid children would have spread in all directions, bearing the fever like gospel. Though he lay as still as death again, sinking to sleep with the pendant in his hand, he knew the day he slept through could offer no resistance. It would end with him as king.

As it happened, Renfield was awake. He started out of sleep about four o'clock every morning, so he could check his trap in peace. He'd rigged a little noose at the high barred window, and he baited it with the loathsome crust of bread they gave him for his dinner. He'd prop his bed against the wall and climb it like a ladder, praying all the while for the food of immortal life. If he was lucky, he got a sparrow or a wren, and he'd tear it down the belly and suck up the blood in a single gulp. If he got his nightly dose, he was sane till midafternoon.

Tonight he was blessed beyond his fondest dreaming. He got up to the window and found a sea gull hanging. He shook so with excitement, he almost dropped it taking it down. It was so fat it could scarcely fit through the bars. He clasped it to his breast and whispered "Thank you, Master" into the night. When he sat in his corner to have it, he practiced his bite on the bird's neck. It took him several tries to sever the vein, and as he drank, he thought he would have to do better. Move more forcefully on the initial attack.

He didn't know when to stop, and it took him an hour to drain the carcass. His stomach was distended, it was so full. He sat in a drunken stupor, the bird in his arms, till the crack of dawn, when he suddenly stirred. He clambered up to the window and moaned with joy. He looked across the harbor square, along the pier to the phantom ship.

"He is here," gasped Renfield, a wave of exultation coursing through him deeper than the blood he'd fed on. "He is here at last, and the dead are free!"

Six

THERE was a pall on the harbor that morning, though at first no one could say why. The fishermen began to take to their boats shortly after dawn, and they were surly with one another, tangling their nets and veering across each other's bows as they sailed out into the open sea. They didn't have to rush. They weren't going to catch any fish today. The mussel gatherers, who came down singing to the harbor pier at eight, with a song about the bounty of the tide, were silent today. They waded out under the pilings guiltily, shivering in the cold. The lighthouse was still lit, and it seemed an ominous thing to see it shining its meaningless light across the day.

The harbormaster, lifting the shade at his office window, was the first to see the *Demeter* lying by the pier. No request had been made in advance for anchorage at Wismar. By law, the captain had to check in with him the instant he landed, and yet there appeared to be no one about. Indeed, the gangplank wasn't even down, nor the ropes secured. It lay there —motionless, alone—and scoffed at the harbor's system. So the harbormaster came outside and knocked on the door of the customs office across the way.

The customs inspector was already dressing down a group of frightened dock laborers, demanding to know the meaning of it. He got no satisfaction. The harbormaster called him, and the two men walked importantly down the pier, fat and righteous and thrilled to have a crisis brewing. A group of curious children had already gathered next to the ship. Two dogs barked without ceasing at the empty deck.

"Put a plank across," the harbormaster ordered the laborers padding along in their train, and the inspector took up the imperious tone. "The ship must be examined thoroughly," he said, "and I will do the job myself."

A plank was brought, and they slung it between the pier and the side of the ship. The inspector and the harbormaster bowed each other across with enormous deference. The decks were silent. They mounted to the bridge and fell against each other squeamishly when they saw Krull's body hanging in the harness, slumped at the wheel. But they steeled themselves and went up close. The harbormaster gripped the body by the hair and turned up the face. The eyes were so wide with horror that they seemed to have sprung the sockets.

"Look!" cried the inspector, pointing a shaking finger at the pulp of puncture wounds on the neck. He staggered away to make his tour of the ship, and the harbormaster, struck with a dread he could not name, stared out across the ship to the unsuspecting town nestled beside the canals. The children called up questions, demanding to know what he'd found. The two dogs on the pier were fighting, tearing at one another's flesh with a strange abandon. The harbormaster waited silently, wishing it all away, till he heard the inspector returning. He knew the news was bad when he saw his ashen face.

"There's not a soul on board," the inspector said. "I found the captain's log, but the last pages make no sense. The writing changes into symbols I can't read." He held up the heavy volume, as if to plead for confirmation, but the harbormaster waited, knowing the worst was still to come. "And the hold," the inspector went on. "I couldn't go down. It is all infested with rats. So many—you can't imagine. I had to shut the door."

"Come," said the harbormaster, leading his comrade away. "We will post quarantine till we have studied the matter further. I think we'd better call the council."

They didn't want anyone panicking, so they made the rounds themselves. The council members agreed to a meeting at noon, in the town hall, and they came through the town at the appointed hour, each from his separate residence, wearing the crimson robes of office. The people in the streets, busy at their labors, looked up in some surprise, since they knew the council didn't meet till the autumn was well advanced. But they shrugged their shoulders and turned again to their work, secure in the knowledge that the course of law was being carried on. A few new laws would only make Wismar a better place to live.

The councillors swept up the stairs to the town hall. They convened in a domed room that looked out on the bustle and cheer of the market square. All about them were models of sailing ships, bearing witness to Wismar's bond with the sea. In the center of the room, lying in state, was the dead captain, whose body had been brought in a covered cart from the pier, down alleys and back streets, so as not to draw attention. Krull was laid out with all the pomp accorded to those whom the sea took victim—dressed in a velvet gown, with a silver cross placed in his folded hands. Doctor van Helsing was bent over the corpse, examining the wound, as the councillors took their high-backed chairs on the dais.

"It baffles me, gentlemen," he testified, when the bailiff gave him the nod. "He has been ravaged repeatedly. I don't understand why he couldn't protect himself. And whatever the beast that bit him, I don't see why it didn't bite him in several places. Why just the neck? I suggest we listen to his last notations in the log."

The harbormaster came forward and laid the heavy book on the lecturn. He opened it like a book of hours, as if he meant to read a sermon or a Psalm. He scanned the page till he found the entry that began the voyage. "Varna, twenty-sixth July," he read with great solemnity. "Course south. Then west to the Dardanelles. The major cargo for the voyage out is a shipment of garden soil for the botanical laboratories in Wismar."

"*What* botanical laboratories?" queried the doctor, but no one spoke in answer. The harbormaster skipped ahead another page and began to read in snatches.

"This morning the fourth man died of fever. Buried at sea. Fourth August—the mate who had the watch last night disappeared without a trace. Fear grows daily among the men, but they will not mutiny. They trust me. Eighth August: seas high. Making fourteen knots toward Biscaya. The first mate throws more bodies over every day. The rats are everywhere."

And now they all waited for him to speak the word. The councillors leaned forward to the edges of their chairs. Once the word was uttered, they knew their power was ended. Pandemonium would be all the rule in Wismar. For this one last moment, each man prayed, against all the mounting evidence, that the sentence wouldn't fall. Outside the windows, in the market square, a hush had swept the crowd, as if everyone felt the first drop of a sudden storm.

"Wednesday, thirteenth August," the harbormaster

read. "The fever has come upon me. I have betrayed the trust of my dearest men. Only the first mate still stands with me. The rats have multiplied again and again. There can be no doubt anymore. It is the plague."

And though they knew it was coming, they all fell back amazed. The councillors tore off their crimson robes and leapt from the dais, shoving their way to the exit. Doctor van Helsing tried to speak, but the harbormaster slapped his face and knocked him down. When the first man burst from the room and reached the town hall stairs, he cried across the market square:

"The plague is upon us! Every man for himself!"

Where were the thousand laws of Wismar now? By the time the doctor struggled out of the domed chamber and down the steps, the crowd was frantic, running away and screaming. The market stalls were tipped, and all the fruit and fish and fresh milk spilled on the cobblestones. The doctor held up his hand to address them. He wanted to announce the rules for the quarantine. He wanted to tell them not to give up hope. But he couldn't be heard above the noise of the crowd, and he stood there all alone.

Around noon, the rats began to creep across the plank. At first, only a few ventured as far as the pier, sniffing and delicate on their feet. Then those few seemed to send back a silent command to the others, urging them to come ahead. The coast was clear. And they came in waves, spilling out of the ship so forcefully that dozens fell from the plank and into the water, squealing and drowning. The numbers were so great, it didn't matter if some died. And the army marching up the plank and across the harbor square didn't register the loss. Food was all they wanted. They'd already smelled the trampled goods a half mile off in the market square.

The proprietor of the harbor cafe was still shuttering his windows when the first pack came. He ran inside, but they were already at his heels, so he couldn't close the door. He had just time to duck into the storeroom closet in his kitchen. Then he listened while they tore at the food on the table. A pot of stew was bubbling on the fire, and the rats jumped up and fell on the coals. They kept on coming and dying, till they piled up body on body, and the next wave was able to reach the iron rim and scoop up the scalding food. The proprietor was nearly out of his mind with the gnashing of their teeth and the smell of burning flesh. But at least he was out of danger, he thought, till he fell against a sack of grain.

All around him were baskets of apples and potatoes. A bin of flour. A side of bacon. The sound had stopped outside in the kitchen, as if the rats had swarmed away and on to the next shop down the street. But he knew they had only finished eating what was out there. And he knew they were waiting, rank on rank, beyond the storeroom door.

No one was in the streets. All the doors were closed. Beside the still canal, the chestnut trees were going yellow, and the nuts grew heavy in the branches. The silence, here in the heat of the midafternoon, was ripe with the promise of harvest in the plains beyond the town. Everything was still in place in certain quarters.

And the bellman came over the bridge, beating his drum with a wooden mallet, the sound as dull as a toothache. He held a document on a scroll, sealed in wax with the mayor's seal. He read it out like the last testament of a doomed race.

"The mayor and councillors of the lawful town of Wismar proclaim the following edict to all good citizens. The plague is landed. It is strictly forbidden, upon pain of imprisonment, to deliver contaminated patients to the hospitals. The dead should be laid down on the banks of the canals. A boat will make hourly rounds to pick them up. The banks are shut till further notice. Each man will have to survive on the stores he has saved up. No provision of any sort will be made by the town of Wismar. This is the last pronouncement till the plague is ended. May God have mercy on you all."

At last the sun went down, but it seemed to grip the horizon at the end, as if to throw a moment more of light. Wismar was deserted. For the moment, the rats were quiet. They had swept the market square and all the gardens and storage bins, but now they burrowed in for the long siege. They crept beneath the bridges and into the stables. They nestled in among the shrubbery. As the sky turned rose and lavender at the fall of dusk, the town lay serene as a still life, full of an early autumn poignancy. It seemed, just now, the perfect place to live. And in every nook and overhang, the rats bunched together in restless sleep, like maggots at a wound.

At the end of a broad and tree-lined avenue, Dracula loomed in the shadows, bent double with the coffin he carried on his back like a curse. He went from house to house, peering at the orderly porches and starched white curtains drawn at the windows. At last he came to an overgrown garden plot surrounding a dark and dilapidated mansion. The doors and windows were boarded shut. It was Red Oaks, and only the darkness stirred inside. No one could remember who'd last lived there, or what the exact history of violence was that attached to its luckless state. But the burghers of Wismar, their dressed-up wives and mannered children, didn't even notice anymore. They walked right by as if they didn't see it.

The vampire walked up the sagging steps, and the boards fell from the door at his approach. The gaslights glowed again in the paneled halls as he made his way to the parlor and eased his burden onto the floor. He scarcely paused to look around him. He had lived in a castle for half a millenium, and he no longer cared for the trappings of property. Or perhaps he knew that the ownership of every house on earth had begun to pass to him, and he didn't need any one place to prove his power. He hastened out of the house again, back to the harbor and the ship. He had a full night's work ahead of him, but as he went through the quiet streets, he couldn't help but thrill with anticipation at the lovely town he'd fallen heir to. He glided along, over the picturesque bridges and by the flowering parks, casting an approving eye. As if he were nothing more than a civic official or a prosperous merchant. As if he planned to live out his life in peace, like any other citizen.

He stood in the harbor square, under the dead of the moon, and sent up a silent hymn of praise to the lordly darkness of the night. At just that moment, a cat came out of the shadows, strutting in his direction. The cat hadn't succumbed to fear when the rats poured in. He had bided his time and pounced when he found a rat that had strayed from the pack. He had had his dinner six times over, and he walked the night with a lilt of pride. But when he saw the vampire, his hair went up on end. He started to back away, hissing with terror.

Dracula reached out and grabbed the cat up in one hand. He held him close against his cloak as he continued across the square, unaware of the scratching and the needlelike teeth of the desperate animal. He came in under the shadow of the hospital, searching along its windows. At last he found the alleyway where the asylum windows faced. Through the bars of one, he could hear the prayer of his visionary priest.

"Oh, Master, make me worthy," Renfield pleaded. "Let me do your work."

And like a father tossing a toy to a fretting child, Dracula reached up and pushed the snarling cat between the bars. He listened to Renfield's moan of pleasure, to the coaxing words he spoke to the terrified cat who huddled in the corner. Then the blow, as Renfield kicked the cat dead against the wall. And the vampire went away feeling proud and just as a doctor, because he kept his people strong.

It was lonely work on the pier, unloading the coffins one by one from the *Demeter*'s hold, bearing them away on his back to his several hiding places. Though he could have walked through the asylum like a healer of souls, releasing all the mad to be his soldiers, he had to do this part himself. The polluted earth in his coffins was the holy ground of his dearest sanctuary. He knew his enemy very well. The light of day was the only shadow across his dream, and his only line of defense was narrow as a grave. He was too shrewd to lose the victory that fluttered in his grasp like a tropical bird. He put down this ring of safety, so he would have a place nearby to run to, wherever the end of the night might find him.

He put a coffin under the drawbridge, deep in the bushes. He put a coffin in the cellar of the windmill. Then one in the town hall dome, at the back of the gallery. One in the bishop's carriage house. He went to the cemetery far at the end of town, where he stowed one in the gardener's shed, and he stood there a moment, ringed with death on every side like a monk in a chapel. And he looked up into the night again, to whisper a lover's promise to it, and saw the black was shot with gray.

The rat's eyes filmed with a thing like tears. He fled out of the graveyard and down the avenue. Though the putting down of his no-man's-land had taken him the whole night, he couldn't go back to the tomb again without a glimpse of Lucy. The light in the sky was mackerel by the time he reached the house beneath the chestnut trees. He crept to the back, where it faced the canal, and climbed the trellis to her bedroom window. The roses died and fell from the vine as his cape drew by them. He pulled himself up to the sill. He saw her.

And though the night fought a losing battle to hold the dawn, though a minute or two would bring a ray of the sun that would seize his skin like a firestorm, he stood there frozen on the topmost rung. He might have been standing there forever and have forever left to go, but he knew no time would ever be enough. Her sleep was dearer to him now than the deepest death. The portrait in the pendant, till now the greatest treasure he'd ever known, was a counterfeit coin compared to this. *I will never let this beauty die,* he thought as he haunted her face with his ruinous gaze. *She will lie with me,* he thought, *and flee this mortal prison.*

It was only the gravity of his oath that could bring him to himself again in time. The light in the sky was gray like a dove when he realized where he was. Crying out in panic, he bounded down from the trellis. He ran along the yard at the edge of the canal, his arms swirling around his head as if to hide in the folds of his cloak. The gray of the sky had shaded into blue, and the horizon in the east was boiling red. He reached the picturesque summer house at the end of Lucy's garden, clawing at his throat and heaving with every breath. He held on to the whitewashed picket fence that ran around it, pulling himself along as if on a crutch. At the back, where the lilac bushes were heavy with shade, he'd broken a hole through to the crawl space underneath, and he dropped to his hands and knees, and crept inside. He did not know how he had the strength to lift the lid of the coffin and climb inside, except he had to for the sake of his beloved. He blacked out almost instantly.

Lucy stared out at the canal. She'd prepared herself for everything, she thought, but it was the silence that unnerved her most. The rats were here, and the infection was blowing about in the air, but it would be another day or so before the people started to drop from it. In the meantime, piercing silence. And now that the sun had dawned on the second day of plague, she was confused about her role in the oncoming battle. Whatever it was she was supposed to do, it wasn't to do with the rats. She'd seen herself somehow acting like a nurse, going from house to house with disinfectants and sleeping powders, facing the horror with the dead and dying. Now she wasn't sure. It seemed to her that she was meant to stay right here and fight it out in her own house.

And she felt somehow, for the first time in several weeks, that she wasn't quite alone. When the cat made an innocent noise, playing with a ball of twine across the room, she whirled around as if a sword had been drawn. She kept going to the door and throwing it wide, as if she heard a crowd in the street outside, or a messenger calling her name. But every time she looked, there was nothing there. Just the chestnut trees in a row, yellow and brown and ready to shed at the first gust of wind. And now she stood in the morning room, a shawl about her shoulders. She couldn't get warm, and she couldn't get out of her mind the cry that had awakened her at dawn. Like the howl of a wolf. Or no: like the howl of a man attacked by wolves.

When she heard the noise of the coach approaching, she stood her ground. It was all in her mind, she thought. She was all alone, no matter how much she felt a presence hovering near. When it stopped in front of the house, she turned and stared at the front door as if daring the phantoms to knock. There was a rap of knuckles against the oak. She clenched her fists and started forward. This was the moment, then. She glanced in the mirror above the horsehair sofa as she went across the parlor to open up. She seemed to want a final glimpse of who she was before the dark encounter caught her up. She had the feeling she'd never look in a mirror again, or never in quite the same way.

The coachman on her doorstep shook with fever, and she thought at first he must want help. She flinched a bit at the heavy breathing that came through the rattle of his throat and filled the entry with contaminated air, but she leaned forward all the same to take his arm. And he shrank from her, shaking his head, and gestured over his shoulder with his thumb. Getting out of the coach was an even sicker man—terribly thin and pasty-faced, and tottering on his legs.

"He says he lives here," the coachman explained, nearly choking on the words.

Oh, my God, she thought. It was Jonathan. She hurried over to him, and he looked up into her eyes with so much pity and defeat that she faltered in all her hope.

"Please," he said, leaning on her arm, "I know there is much between us, madam. I have seen your face before. But I can't remember when. If you will only have a little patience, and tell me all you know, I will soon be good as new."

He spoke with enormous dignity and courage. She held him in her arms, frail and sickly, and told herself she had to endure it. *This is not the worst,* she thought. At least he was back alive. The two of them moved together toward the house, and she turned to beckon the coachman to follow.

"No, ma'am," he said, looking about deliriously. "I must fly this cursed and soundless town. There is darkness on your house." And he wheeled abruptly and staggered drunkenly back to the waiting vehicle. He heaved himself up in the seat and flicked the reins. The horses took off at a gallop. He didn't seem to understand that it didn't matter where he fled. The darkness was inside him now.

126

At the doorway, Jonathan stopped. She looked over at him questioningly. In his upturned hand was a yellow leaf, and he stared up into the tree that shaded the house. She followed his gaze. The leaves had begun to fall like rain. Within an hour the trees would be black and bare.

In the alleys of Wismar, paved with stones, the rats erupted without any warning. They would storm along like a spring tide—foraging, always foraging—and then, just as suddenly, disappear into the cellar holes and dumps of refuse. Some men had not even seen them yet. Some men swore it was all a rumor. But the streets were empty as death, because no one would venture out alone to see.

Except the goldsmith. He had sat inside long enough. He told his wife he still had work to do, no matter if the town had taken leave of its senses and declared an illegal holiday. If he was meant to catch the plague, then so be it. But in the meantime, he intended to get a little more work done. Besides, he knew that rats did not eat people. They wanted food, and they were satisfied to comb the garbage and be left in peace. They were more afraid of men than not.

So he walked through the quiet streets to his shop on the market square, fearful there may have been vandals looting. But everything was tidy and in its place. He weighed out an ounce of gold dust to calm his nerves, furious at the disbanding of the police and the closure of the banks. The business of daily life ought to go on as usual, he thought, plague or not. There was no town, no civilized life at all, if the shops were shut and the merchants were all barricaded in their homes.

He put the dust back in the safe. He ran an idle hand through a bowl of wedding rings. What kind of a town was this, he thought, where even the vandals had locked themselves in? It gave him a sudden idea. He grabbed up his kit of jeweler's tools and stepped out into the ghostly square. He crossed among the broken stalls, where every scrap and morsel had been taken, to the great stone temple of the Merchants' Bank.

He ducked around the side and came along into the alley behind. The back door sported a simpleton's lock. He set his kit down on the cobblestones and went to work with an instrument delicate as a surgeon's. The guards were all at home. The law was over.

He was right about rats, of course. They would have been perfectly glad to settle for garbage covered with flies and stinking. But they'd already eaten their way through all of that, and still they raved with hunger. They'd started to eat the flowers. They'd cornered all the stray cats and dogs. The spiders and worms and beetles had vanished in their train. So they couldn't resist the smell of so much meat in the alley. They flowed out of all their hiding places, little mouths agape.

The goldsmith turned in horror, first to the left, then to the right. They came at him without any anger, their eyes all glazed, and they reached his feet and pulled him down at the very moment he sprang the lock. He fell over onto the marble floor of the bank. They covered him in a swarm. He only screamed a moment, because the kings and the warrior rats were at his throat from the first. With so many to feed, it was over in minutes. The bones lay white and curiously chaste on the cold stone. And the rats went nuzzling about the bank, dulled with their dinner. Utterly unimpressed by the scope of Wismar's treasure.

It was nearing the end of the afternoon when Schrader brought Mina to the Harkers' house. Lucy had finally succeeded in making Jonathan comfortable. She had first propped him up in an armchair in the morning room, but he complained that the sun gave him a headache. She finally bedded him down on the sofa in the parlor, and she drew the drapes and kept a cold cloth on his eyes, till at last he dozed and his breathing grew more rhythmic. Whenever he was conscious, she fed him sips of tea so full of milk and honey that it spooned like syrup. And all the while she lullabied him with his history. All he seemed to know was who he was, Jonathan Harker of Wismar. She repeated the thousand details of their life together. She told him all about his job. She avoided mentioning anything to do with the journey that had broken him. By the time the clock on the mantel chimed the hour at four o'clock, he was smiling bravely and calling her by name.

When Schrader burst in, nearly frantic with worry, he scarcely seemed to register the fact that Jonathan was home. Mina stood back in the shadows, surrounded by the fallen leaves and mumbling to herself.

"Help us, Lucy," Schrader cried. He drew her to the door and gestured at his wife where she waited outside. "She speaks in tongues, and she calls the rats from the stable yard like kittens. She *feeds* them, Lucy! They eat out of her hand!"

"Bring her in," said Lucy calmly.

"It's no use," her brother answered. "She will not enter your house. She says it's full of evil. What are we going to do? They'll take her away and lock her up like Renfield!"

"No, they won't. No one is going to lock anyone up till the plague is done. What else does she say?"

"She says she is an angel," Schrader replied, and he buried his face in his hands and wept. Lucy drew him into the house and brought him through to the dining room. She could see the look of fear on Jonathan's face, and she didn't want to upset him further. She poured out a glass of brandy for Schrader, then went to coax Mina inside. The street outside the house was empty, but she didn't try to follow. She was seized again with the certainty that her duty lay with those

129

who'd come within her sanctuary. If Mina was an angel, as she said, then God would keep her safe.

"She said she would meet you at home," Lucy explained to her brother, and when he tried to rise and go, she laid a hand on her arm and shook her head. "No. You must let her seek the answer she has waited for. It is more than fever in Wismar now."

"But, Lucy, how will it end? Will we wake one morning to find ourselves bound in straitjackets?"

"All we can do," she said, "is love one another as best we can. We must give up everything else."

He was a man of business, not a lover. He would rather have grappled a monster. But he seemed to know what she meant, because he got a grip on himself and stood up proudly.

"But that is why, dear Lucy, I must go to Mina. Even though she flees me."

"It may be your death," she warned.

"So be it, then," he said, and they went arm in arm to the door. The dusk had already fallen outside. There were sounds of animals calling, and it seemed they would tear each other to pieces when the night pressed in. Lucy wanted to beg him now to wait till morning, but she knew it was no use. She couldn't protect her brother anyway, because he had his own appointment with it. She couldn't hold him back from his battle with a madwoman, not if that was the only way he could die of love.

They embraced like brother and sister severed by a war. She watched him go off into the dark, and only the worried sound of Jonathan's voice could break the reverie that followed on his parting. She was glad to have something concrete to go to. She smoothed his brow with the cool cloth and held her hands against his cheeks till he fell asleep again. She knew less now about what she was to do than she'd known a day or two ago. But she had no fear of the unknown, as long as she could stand on her own ground. This quiet time in the candlelight, cradling the man she loved so he rested and got well, was a dream she would have risked her life to bring about. And now that she had it, she knew the hour was fast upon her when she would have to pay. Well, let it come. With Jonathan home, she knew exactly what it was she was fighting for.

And out beyond the roses, at the bottom of Lucy's garden, Mina danced in a slow circle, welcoming the night. She was hardly in this world at all anymore. For days she had watched her husband from the edge of heaven, and she only consented to walk among these mortals in order to make an example. The people of Wismar needed to see why they must cling to their perfection. Glory waited just ahead of them. It fountained in their midst, now that the army of holy innocents had arrived.

Her pain was like a choir in a cathedral, more exquisite with every step she danced. She capered through the roses, stopping once to wrap her hand around a long stem spiked with thorns, thrilling to its kiss as she pulled it off the bush. And then she saw the rats waiting on the rails of the summer house. She let out a mild and motherly sound of pleasure and went toward them. She opened the gate in the picket fence and went up three wooden steps to the circular porch.

They were ringed all around her on the railing, looking up into her rapturous face. Through the window of her agony, they seemed to her like a flock of doves. She was meant, like a saint, to teach them a song of infinite peace. She hummed a fragment from out of her childhood, something she played on a harpsichord when she and the world were virgin ground. She went around the floor, waltzing, and she put out her free hand to the innocents, and they kissed the tips of her fingers.

She lacked nothing in this world. She scooped up a

131

squealing rat and held it close against her heart. She stood at the rail and looked out along the garden, wishing only that she had someone to tell it to. Someone who had reached the same high place. And when she heard the sweep of the cape behind her, felt the breath on her neck, she knew her prayer had reached the throne, and God himself had come to hear her sing. She opened her arms as she turned around, and the rose fell to the floor, and the rat leapt down. The face that loomed in the darkness was more beautiful than her dreams of it could ever express. The eyes were old as the earth and deeper than the night. She could have died from the joy of it, because she saw that he wanted *her*.

She threw her head back, and the vampire took her. This one kiss, she knew, was a thousand times more ravishing than all the love on earth could gather up. She was God's bride. She swirled her hands in the folds of his cloak, and they danced that way till she fell over into heaven.

It must have been the middle of the night before Lucy felt she could safely leave her husband's side and go upstairs to bed. He had been beset with nightmares, almost from the moment he closed his eyes, and there didn't seem anything she could do but hold his hand while he fought his monsters. She stayed because she loved him, but she found herself listening closely to all he said. A lot of it was disjointed and incoherent. She lost the thread of it every time he got close to the horror that had marked him so. But she was able to piece together enough of a picture from his raving and pleading to know what the castle looked like and how the evil felt that lurked within. When at last poor Jonathan had been quiet for an hour, she rose from the sofa convinced that the Count stood at the center of all this sorrow and pain.

She snuffed the lamps and mounted to her room. The kitten was on her dresser, playing with her combs, and she watched her as if it would clear her mind. When she opened her jewel case and took off her bracelets, the kitten leapt up to the side, eager to find a new toy. She put out a paw and tangled a thin gold chain before Lucy could move to stop it. She pushed the animal away, and the chain came with it. Suddenly, there on the linen cloth, was the tiny cross she'd worn on her wedding day. On an impulse she hardly understood, she unwrapped the chain from the kitten's paw. She undid the clasp and drew it round her neck so the cross hung down on her bodice. She looked in the mirror, and for a moment it seemed to take her back to when she was a girl.

But the moment passed when the kitten arched her back and began to snarl and spit at something behind her. Lucy felt the presence of darkness, but she was too horror-struck to turn and face it. She stared at her own eyes in the mirror, then looked off to either side. There was nothing there. Except for the cat, she was all alone. She began to shake, and she knew it was worse than her worst nightmare if she couldn't see it in the glass. She leaned up close to the mirror and touched her cheek against the cool of her own image, as if she meant to tumble through to safety. In the room beyond the mirror, the horror could not follow.

"Lucy?" the vampire said quite softly—shyly, even, as if he weren't sure that he'd said it right. "You must excuse my coming in unbidden, but I—cannot always stop myself. I am—"

And he paused before he told her who he was. It seemed, though she couldn't see him, that he grappled to put it gently. He might have been ashamed of his own name. Or he wasn't worthy of her somehow. *Remember that,* she told herself. It might prove to be the only weapon she had against him.

"—Count Dracula," she whispered.

"Ah," he said, "then you know. It is so much easier, that way."

"I know you have done my husband great harm," she said coldly, lifting her cheek from the mirror again and looking in at the empty room behind her. The cat had stopped her hissing. Now she sat and stared with glassy eyes at the vampire; her mouth hung open as if she had slipped under a spell. Was that what would happen to Lucy when she turned? Would it all be over so fast? It pricked the anger in her. "So," she went on, "it does no use to come to me. I can only hate you."

"Your husband will not die," the vampire replied. About the other, Lucy's hatred, it seemed he would kill himself with grieving. But he spoke not a word to plead his sentence.

"He *will*," she snapped, "and then I will curse your name forever! But till he slips away from me, I will count each moment left to us more precious than a kingdom."

"Jonathan Harker is a lucky man," said Dracula. "With so much love between you, perhaps you have more than you need. Perhaps you would let a lonely man—partake of some."

"*Never,*" she seethed, and the rage was so great that she turned without fear. Hideous though he was, she saw with a thrill of triumph that he was no more than what he said—a lonely man. "Nothing can ever violate the bond between us. If he never knew my face again, I would keep that bond, for both our sakes."

But Dracula hardly seemed to listen. He retreated away to the bed and grabbed hold of the post and swayed. He pointed a shivering finger at her heart, and then he began to gasp. She looked down at the shining cross. As soon as she understood the nature of the power, she made a quick decision and put up a hand to hide it. She waited while he recovered his breath again. She knew he could have run out of the room to escape it, the moment he saw it, but neither one of them had quite finished speaking.

"Thank you," he said, and in spite of herself she felt a pang at the misery in his hollow eyes. "What I am trying to say, Lucy, is that I could change everything. Whatever you wanted. Your husband could be saved. The plague could go away as quickly as it came. If you would only come to me and be my friend."

"Why do you want to hurt me? What have I never done to you?"

"Hurt you? *Hurt* you?" He bellowed as he did in his own castle, like a trapped animal, and here in Lucy's bedroom it seemed as if the walls would crack. She trembled, but she stood her ground. Her hand lay still on her breast and covered the cross. "You speak of death with so much anger," Dracula said, coming toward her in the center of the room. "Lose it, then. I will make you immortally young, Lucy. Queen of the night forever."

She looked away sadly—not so much to dismiss the gift he offered as to indicate she didn't know what to say. She knew one thing: she wasn't terrified in the least. To come to her, he had struggled to keep his human side. He possessed himself so closely for a moment only, at the midpoint of the night. He left his terrors ravening out in the dark. They were equals here.

"Perhaps it is more cruel not to die," she said. "One would have no reason to seize life, if one never had to risk it. You—are *you* alive?"

"I suffer. Isn't that enough?"

"I know you are in pain," she said, looking up at him. He was standing so close she could feel his cape along one arm. "But you suppose it is only I who can help you. There you're wrong. Salavation is in ourselves alone."

"Is it God you speak of?" asked the vampire in disdain. He had heard the nicest arguments before.

"No," she said. And thought: if he is only evil, he will take me in the midst of my denial. "God is much like you, I think. Alone, I mean. And of course, He loves the world."

"I love *you*," the vampire said, and the cape surrounded her as he drew her close. He bent his open mouth to kiss her throat—to kiss it only, not to sting. She felt herself let go. She was saved by such a little thing. Her limp hand fell away numbly from her heart as she collapsed, and the cross so close to his face burned the vampire's lips like a splash of acid. A wolf's moan broke from his throat. Anyone else, and he would have dropped her like a curse and run. But she might have hurt herself falling. Though he strangled and heaved with nausea, he swept her up in his arms and over to her bed. He laid her down and groped away to the door.

Suffocation twisted up his lungs. His eyes were so raw with the burning that he could hardly see the shape of her in bed. But he stood one moment more and watched, as if he would guard her the whole night long. As if he were the last thing she should fear. And when he was sure he heard her breathing deeply, fast asleep, he turned and stumbled down the stairs. He went over to Jonathan for a drink. But something stopped him, even here, and he knew he had to flee this house. He had to kill a hundred women, before the crack of dawn, to quiet the wildness that threatened to shake his power to bits.

Seven

THE fever struck during the night. A morning fog had settled on the town, and several people gathered on the hospital steps to clamor for medicine that didn't exist. Doctor van Helsing came out to try to comfort them, but they preferred to be enraged. They accused him and all the authorities of Wismar of hiding the truth about the contamination till it was too late to flee to high country. They accused him of having a cure he was saving for the rich. They were half of them fevered themselves. They would have thrown eggs and overripe fruit, but they didn't dare waste a morsel of food.

The doctor stumbled back in and sadly gave the word to his guards to disperse the crowd. He fled to his office, covering his ears against the cries of people beaten and defeated, sent home empty-handed. The situation was grave and would be graver still with every hour that passed. Five hundred, perhaps, had been stricken already, and they were well into the first stage—chills and high fever, hallucinations, loss of appetite. The town was still on its ghastly holiday.

137

The whole municipal apparatus had been disbanded. Doctor van Helsing still had a staff about him at the hospital, but only because the nurses and guards felt safer there, as if on sanctified ground. It was all an illusion, of course. There was no safe place in Wismar.

The doctor knew he could do nothing now but wait. In two or three days, thousands would have passed the crisis of the third stage. Then they would have enough dead to heap in a charnel house, but there would also be some few survivors—a quarter of the town if they were lucky. And it was for those few that the hospital was being kept ready, to nurse them back to health from their weakened state. But van Helsing couldn't help but wonder, as he sat in his office without any skill to help the suffering in Wismar, if the crowd wasn't right. If he'd listened to Lucy from the very beginning, couldn't he have ensured the evacuation of the children, at least? He looked out of his window, across the square to the empty schoolhouse, and wept for the fate of his fellow man.

Lucy came in unannounced, her manner grave and purposeful. She waited in the doorway till he'd finished crying. When he looked up, weary and defeated, she went to his desk and spread out her plans for the neighborhood hospitals. Her knowledge of the course of the plague was impressive, and her scheme for the recuperative period was more sophisticated than van Helsing's own. He began to feel hope again as he listened to the calm in Lucy's voice.

"I blame myself," he said when she had finished.

"No," she replied. "We are all to blame. But I think it may still be possible to stop this horror at the source."

"What do you mean?" he asked. She was scanning among his shelves, looking through his books for something she had only cast a glance at when she was here before. After a moment, she pulled out a heavy volume. She laid is down on the desk, and he read the word that burned across the cover: *Nosferatu.*

"Jonathan chants this word whenever the fever is high," she explained. "I have listened to all his delirious memories. He has had dealings with a vampire."

"No such thing," the doctor replied with a firm shake of his head. "If you read every book on these shelves, Lucy, you would see that the superstitions of the past have begun to yield to the enlightment of science. There is a long way yet to go, but the terrors of the darkness have at last been engaged. Your husband suffers from the plague. Do not get caught up in delusions."

"I am absolutely certain," she said. "I have seen the vampire with my own eyes."

"Your husband's illness has worn you out. You must go home and rest." He would not listen. He knew the hysterical theories would be starting up around the town. But he expected more control from Lucy, who'd had the courage to see the plague coming from the moment the first rumors had reached Wismar. Now that he'd seen the plans she drew up for the care of survivors, he wanted to appoint her as his assistant in the coming struggle. He couldn't afford to have her playing with will-o'-the-wisps.

"I beg you, doctor. Help me to crush this monster." If she had to do it alone, she knew she would surely die. Doctor van Helsing was her last chance. "Jonathan says he has brought coffins filled with polluted earth, by sea from Varna. I think he had hidden them all over Wismar, to hide himself from the light of the day. If you will only help me find them, we can kill him in his lair. But we must search them out *now*, while he still sleeps. Tonight, it will be too late. Tonight, he comes to take me."

While she spoke, she trembled with dread. The doctor concluded there was nothing he could do. She had the fever now herself. He came around his desk and held her in his arms, silently cursing the darkness that had swept her up. He could only humor her now.

"Of course, my dear, of course. You go on home. I will come to you as soon as I have finished getting ready here." In a couple of hours, he knew, she would be too weak to leave her bed. This hallucination would pass, and another would take its place. "I will bring a stake to drive into the vampire's heart," he lied, "and together we will track him down."

He led her out to the hallway and instructed his most trusted guard to see her home. Her eyes were dull as she walked away. She knew he had not believed her. She carried the book of vampires under one arm and cast an agonized look at the town she would have to save on her own. Every hour, the situation grew more extreme. The rats would overrun a house without any warning, crushing against the doors in such vast numbers that they broke inside. They ate up all the food and mangled anyone trapped within. Reports were abroad in the town that a hundred women had died in the night, from fear alone.

When they crossed the canal and came along the chestnut alley in front of Lucy's house, she dismissed the guard quite curtly. She was turning to go inside when she heard a shriek from the garden. She thought the rats had taken the house next door, and she fumbled with the key in the lock, though she knew she had nothing to fear for herself. There was an invisible zone of protection around her. It was Jonathan she had to keep safe.

But before she could hasten inside, Schrader appeared from the side of the house, staggering out of the garden. He was holding his dead wife in his arms, and he wailed with pain, though he didn't seem to see Lucy at all. He wandered the dangerous night all alone. The rats had nipped at his feet wherever he walked, and he kicked them away and strangled them in his bare hands. Twice he was seized with a sense of overwhelming danger, so he hid behind trees while the vampire passed in shadow. Nothing stopped his searching. Though Mina had taken a darker lover, he bore all the love he had like a beacon and tried to find her in time to save her. Just after dawn, he fainted from exhaustion in a deserted street. The rats were around him in a ring, the moment he hit the ground, but the raging love inside him held them back. They let him alone and went for choicer prey.

But what good did it do him now? He swore revenge against the indifferent sky and buried his anguished face in Mina's neck. That is when Lucy, helpless to give him comfort, noticed the two ripe puncture wounds on the side of Mina's throat, the last of the blood crusted around them. It was not fever, then. Nor madness, either. She clutched her book more tightly as she recalled the two white scars on Jonathan's throat.

Her brother walked away beneath his burden, hearthbroken and alone, without so much as a word of recognition. She tried to banish the image from her mind as she came in and called to her husband. But the hope that he might not have heard the commotion fled when she saw his somber face.

"He came to tell us what he saw in his travels through the town," said Jonathan grimly, raising his head from the pillow. "All is lost. The plague has reached as far as Riga. The fever there is one day advanced ahead of ours. They roast their pets in the street. A baby has been born with the head of a rat." He looked at her with the strangest glare of accusation, as if to demand what words of relief she dared speak now. "He said he believed that Mina had fled to the countryside, that the country air would calm her nerves. When the world ends,

141

Lucy, does a man only lie to himself? He told me all these terrors, all the while convincing himself they wouldn't come to him. And then he glanced out the parlor window, and he *saw* her!"

Jonathan pointed a bony finger toward the garden, then fell back and closed his eyes, weary from so much talking. Lucy didn't know what to say. She could not assure him that every pair of lovers in Wismar wouldn't end just as tragically, just as far apart. What she hadn't expected was this distance in him. She'd prepared for a thousand agonies, her death included—but not for losing Jonathan. Late the night before, she'd defied the vampire. She said she could love enough for two if Jonathan couldn't return it. But could she? And could she go off to the weird, unspeakable meeting with the darkness if she weren't secure in Jonathan's love?

She sat by the fire, very near him, and turned the pages of the vampire book. In a moment, she knew he would sink into sleep, and then he would start to murmur the tale of his journey once again. It came in no particular order, and gypsies and nuns were mixed in together with innkeepers, coachmen, and wolves. But she'd heard out all the scenes with the Count, and she saw the lonely castle very clearly. She knew he had snatched up her pendant. Knew that he slept in a tomb beneath a dome. Things that Jonathan didn't even know he knew, he babbled out of his haunted dream.

But as the dream had not yet started, she found herself drawn to the language of dread that filled the book in her lap. *"Nosferatu,"* she whispered when she saw the name. God of the Undead. He is as a shadow, and he makes no mark on a mirror. Abandon hope, all whom he approaches." She turned the page. She felt she had read these things before, a long time past. Softly, to herself, she read aloud the antidote. "Though the vampire be an unnatural being, he must obey some natural laws. The sign of the cross bans him. A consecrated host will bar his retreat. If a woman pure of heart should make him forget the cry of the cock, the first light of day will destroy him forever."

She looked out the parlor window, down the sun-shot garden to the summer house at the far end. She didn't see any way out. She would have to court him all night long, and trick him into staying past his time. Curious, how it made her calm. Now that she knew the specific task, she saw she would simply *have* to survive it. There was so much despair and madness in Wismar now, the people might not know the horror was over unless she came back to tell them.

"Why?" cried Jonathan out of his sleep, fighting to get away from a thing he couldn't name. "Why?"

"Because," she said, looking out on the fallen leaves and speaking half to herself, "we've forgotten the dark side of nature. That is why. It has not forgotten us."

Renfield sat in his cell, cooing over a rat he held in his arms. The rat would not purr for him like a cat, but it made no move to bite or escape. It had appeared at his window as if by design, and it waited till Renfield climbed up to lift it down. Renfield took it as a sign of his Master's favor. It was time to go. He could not reason anymore, so he couldn't make a plan. He scarcely knew where he was, or what town lay outside beyond the bars, so far had the madness knotted up his brain. But he was ready to walk through the walls, if need be. His Master had work for him to do.

He heard the one-eyed warden coming down the hall, accompanied by a burly guard. It was time for Renfield's supper, but of course the tray of slops was only an excuse. The guard would hold him down while the warden beat him. It had been this way for days, though Renfield couldn't remember. He let the rat down on the floor and batted it away with his foot. He began to scream as the key turned in the lock.

"Coming Mr. Renfield, coming," called the warden through the grill, beside himself with expectation.

But when the two men shouldered in, they were struck quite dumb with horror. Renfield held his foot as if he'd had a bite, and a rat maybe two feet long crouched in the middle of the cell floor. Now they didn't care a whit for the madman, but the rat threw them into confusion. The hospital had so far managed to keep itself clear of vermin, and they clung to the notion that the plague could not enter the walls if the rats were all outside. They did not understand that the infection was in every breath of air they breathed.

"Beat him, Jack," the warden cried, and the guard brought his stick down hard on the rat's spine, again and again, as the rat tried to creep back into the corner. In a moment it fell over dead, and the two men came up close to see. With a thrill of triumph, they peered at the enemy that had found its match at last.

Renfield howled like a wolf, and the two men whirled in time to see him jump. He landed on the warden and threw him down on the floor—just as he'd done before, only this time he went for the neck. He bit clean through the jugular, with a wondrous surgical precision, before the guard could move to separate them. And then, on the stroke of the same moment, the guard heard a low growl behind him and turned to the horror of the rat's leap.

It was an awesome partnership. The rat had as his reward the mauling of the guard. He ran up and down the screaming man, biting and digging in his claws. Renfield, meanwhile, couldn't suck up all the blood in time. It fountained out all over him. But though it spilled and spread on the floor, he drank his fill. The taste of it drove him wild with pleaure.

And when they were done, they disengaged themselves from their prey and came out of the cell together. Renfield pulled the door shut behind him. They walked the hall on soundless feet, where a moment before the warden and guard had clumped along, and behind each door the mad woke up. They sidled up to the barred windows and reached out hands as if to touch a passing god. Renfield, spattered with the warden's blood, smiled his blessing on either side and drifted by. He climbed the stairs with the rat at his side and reached the hospital doors without encountering any resistance. The place was deserted. It was as if the staff had busied itself in all the remotest parts of the building so as not to have to face this shadow of darkness within its midst.

Renfield walked out, a free man again. The rat took off down the stairs and away across the square, his mission done. And Renfield went among his people. He saw a plague cart stacked with coffins, ready for the crisis when the fever reached its peak and the numberless dead would have to be hauled away. He saw the vandals looting the shops, stealing goods they would have no use for now. At the corner of two streets, he watched a man strangle a woman, but he was too crazy to say if it was pity or rage in the man's dead eyes. He saw a pack of children setting fires, going from house to house with torches. Perhaps it was an act of cleansing.

And wherever Renfield went, nobody paid him any mind. They didn't find it the least bit odd, to see a man streaked with blood. He saw a man beset by rats, pleading for help as they clambered up his trousers. Because Renfield's mind was gone, he didn't know the man was a bishop. The random nature of the rats' attacks made as much sense as anything. He saw the people run the other way when one of their fellow townsmen was surrounded, and he thought it was normal, everyday behavior. Nobody cared what happened to anyone else. Each rabid citizen of Wismar willed himself to survive, and each saw the others as nothing more than a pool of victims lengthening his chances. One man's agony was the next man's narrow escape. And in the blank of Renfield's head, it was all the given of life at large.

But though he felt quite at home, he knew he was only a spectator here. He was passing the time till the fall of dark, when he would meet his master. He would have to go abroad and prepare the way, so he wouldn't be staying here. But meanwhile he walked with the proud and easy gait of a gentleman out for his Sunday constitutional. A man leaned out a window and vomited in the street. A woman ran up on a bridge and tossed her baby into the canal. The rats chased a horse into an alley and brought it down. It was all quite lovely, Renfield thought. It seemed to him like a town where nothing ever went wrong.

Lucy stood at the window, watching the sun go down. When it slipped below the horizon, far out acrooss the plains, she began to move swiftly. She took up her jewel box, threw on her darkest cloak over a midnight velvet dress, and hastened across the parlor to bid her sleeping husband goodbye. She knelt and shook him by the shoulder, calling his name. She had let him sleep all afternoon.

"You must wake up," she said. "You must not sleep again till I return."

"Where are you going? demanded Jonathan, squinting through a splitting headache. He acted as if she were abandoning him.

"I have an errand," she replied. She kissed his

pouting lips, smoothed a hand across his forehead, and waited till he nodded. "I love you," she said, but he made no answer.

She hurried across the darkening town, trying to keep her mind on nothing else but the steps of her plan. She ignored the coroner, going from door to door in his tophat and tails, knocking to see who was still alive. If no one answered his knock, he chalked the door with a white cross. She ignored the fistfights and the cries for help. When she saw a bonfire up ahead, where a neighborhood threw on its furniture piece by piece, she detoured down an alley. All along her way, she heard the rustle and squeal of the rats, but she didn't flinch and didn't stop.

It was her second errand of the day. A few hours earlier, she had left the house and made the rounds of the city churches. Every one was empty. No one was praying in Wismar now, and even the priests appeared to have given up. She thought she might have to plead for help, but she found she could walk up boldly to the altar without anyone detaining her. She found the consecrated wafers in a silver dish to the left of the cross, and without any ceremony, she spilled them into the empty jewel cask she carried with her. Before she left each altar, she would stare for a moment at each cross, as if to pay her respects, however briefly. There was a time when she would have said a prayer as well, but that whole part of her heart was no longer convinced. The incarnation of evil hadn't sent her back to a deeper faith in God. The only one she trusted absolutely was herself.

At last she came to the ruined mansion—Red Oaks. She walked up the swaying steps, across the porch. The door was already open, looking as if it had sagged on its hinges for years, but when she crossed the threshold, it slammed behind her horribly. She didn't startle for an instant. She went along the hallway, peering into the dusk and cobwebs. It was the scurrying of rats in the parlor that drew her in. She advanced to the center of the room, and there lay the coffin, its lid ajar. The odor of dank and mildew overwhelmed her.

She put out a hand and slid the lid aside, but it was empty except for the mound of soil. She opened her cask and pulled out a handful of wafers. She crushed them in palm as she made a circle round the bier, sprinkling the crumbs in a ring. She could hear the rats grow furious in the corners of the room. She knew it was only one of many he'd secreted about town, but if her plan worked, this was the coffin he would flee to at daybreak. When he found the way barred here, there wouldn't be time to run to the next.

All through the house, the rats seethed to get at her. But they made no move, having had the word from a higher power that she was to be spared—even if she meant to murder him. She left the broken mansion and made her way home through the ravaged streets. She didn't know how many hours she had to wait, but she knew he would not fail to come. There were facets of the night where her power far exceeded his. She would not hesitate to use it.

Dracula emerged into the twilight, the wings of his great black cape aswirl with power. He had passed the day in the gardener's shed in the graveyard, and as soon as he stepped out of his coffin, the smell of death came over him like a burst of winter flowers. He drifted about among the graves like a kind of gardener himself, and at last he came to the halfway house, by the main gate. Here the first victims of the fever had already been brought, perhaps twenty in all—the old and feeble whom the plague swept off before it had half begun. And here the palsied undertaker would pretty them up to lie in their coffins. He would have to work in dreadful haste, because by this time tomorrow the corpses would be stacked on every side like cords of wood.

Dracula entered the undertaker's workroom, thinking to make a body count. He had no thought of taking supper here, hungry though he was. There was better blood to be had all over Wismar—virgin's blood and baby's blood, vivid as nectar and pure as the deepest water. He only wanted to know how well the plague was doing. He was surprised, therefore, to see another figure bent to a corpse and drinking. His heart lifted at the thought of a brother vampire come to share the bounty. But when he stepped forward and flapped his cape in greeting, the naked ghoul fell back from the corpse, looked up astonished at Dracula's face, and prostrated himself on the stone floor like a worshipper. It was only Renfield.

"You have developed a taste for the night, I see," the vampire said.

"Forgive me, Master," Renfield pleaded, trembling at the majesty all about him. "I do not mean to overstep my place."

"Not at all. Not at all. Stand up before me."

And the madman rose and faced him. He gazed upon the vampire's empty eyes, the pale skin of his bald and bulbous head, the bat's ears and grim lips. His life had come to something great. He was a prophet standing before his god, and there was nothing he wouldn't do to extend his Master's power. He longed to give up his life, because he knew he would enter a state more perfect even than death. And the vampire felt his act of worship. He was so accustomed to fear and screaming that he had no words to speak his joy. If Renfield loved him, Lucy might. It did not have to be horror and torture.

"Tell me what to do," begged Renfield, breaking the silence. He still seemed fearful that he had offended.

"We must become brothers in blood," said Dracula. "Kiss my hand." And he reached his clawed and icy fingers toward the naked man, inviting him to drink.

"I can't. I am not worthy," he said, beginning to shake with the wildness of it. The vampire reached out farther. There was no denying him. Renfield opened his mouth and put it around three fingers of Dracula's hand. He bit down gently and closed his eyes in prayer.

"Take it, take it," whispered the vampire, and Renfield bit down harder. As the taste of the vampire's polluted blood filled his mouth, he felt as if he had stepped off a precipice, into the air. He hovered like an angel over a darkness deeper than any he had ever known, and the corpses in the charnel house writhed around him, even in death. Nothing would ever be the same. He withdrew his mouth and looked down humbly at the floor, too overcome with happiness to meet the vampire's gaze.

"Now yours," commanded Dracula, and Renfield held up his hand in turn—meekly, shyly, as if a king had asked to knight him. The vampire brought him closer and bent to his wrist. The two fangs sank in expertly, right into the vein, and tapped it like a spring. But only for a moment. The vampire wasn't out to feed. He was true to the ceremony of the occasion, and he drew back soberly. They were comrades in the kingdom now. Dracula did not seek to be a tyrant.

"Go north to Riga," he said. "The Black Death shimmers in the air. The army of rats awaits your command. I will follow as soon as Wismar falls. A day or two at most."

"Thy will be done," said Renfield, full of awe and glory. He padded across the deathroom and bowed at the door. He turned to go.

"One other thing," said Dracula. "What can you tell me of Lucy Harker?"

Renfield stared as if it struck no chord. But after a

moment, he felt the shadows part, and a face swam out of the murk in his head. He could no longer remember who he used to be before he went mad, and he did not connect the name with the woman who had visited him in his cell. He didn't know what she used to be to him. He couldn't think of a thing to say, and yet the Master waited for his word, so he must speak.

"She used to tease me," he said.

She waited in her bedroom, as before. She had no idea what hour of the night it was by the clock. The clocks had all stopped the day before, and she had made no move to wind them. She only knew sunset and dawn now, and she knew just how much time there was before first light, as if it were a length of rope she was winding in. Her cat sat by her on the bed, her eyes as glazed as they had been the previous night, when Dracula had appeared. As Lucy patted her gently, she could see how peaceful madness was. No wonder the travelers to that country hardly ever came back. There was no fever there.

The vampire came on soundless feet. She was aware of his presence by the slightest drop in temperature, as if the wind had turned outside. But she did not raise her eyes until he spoke. Mentally, she started the countdown until the rising sun.

"How very becoming you are in black," he said.

"I wear it," she said as she stood and faced him, "for all the sorrow that has come to Wismar. I have thought all day about what you said. Tell me what it is you want."

"Come into the night and live with me," he pleaded. He noticed she was not wearing her cross. As she swept by him toward the dresser, he instinctively stepped back, out of her way. She stood at the mirror, brushing her long black hair while she talked.

"But why would I ever trust *you*?" she demanded. "You have brought us nothing but pain."

"Have I?" he asked, his dead hands folded and mute above his heart. "Is it *I* who must bear the blame? Isn't it rather the nature of things? Your city of laws— so perfect, so removed from chaos—does it not command me to exist?"

"That is all *talk*!" she snapped, shaking the brush in his face. The silence grew as she chose from among her jewels spilled across the dresser. She tried a topaz on a chain against her throat. Then a string of pearls. Finally she settled on a cameo, which he watched her clasp around her neck with a hunger that knew no end.

"Still," she said coyly, "I would consider your offer, even so, except I know so little about—what you are."

"You know all the superstitions, don't you?" He was angry and bitter beneath his courtly air, because the gift he had to give her had no expression in any human tongue. "Only the Undead know the rest. But we are beings wholly without illusions. We pity you who are trapped in time. Men are all full of hope for tomorrow, and tomorrow is when they die. Eternity makes a man a realist."

He could tell he had reached her. She was quiet a moment, and she looked in the mirror as if she couldn't trust it anymore. It didn't give every answer plain. She turned and held out a hand.

"May I take your arm, then?" she asked, and he stumbled forward to do her bidding, he whom the whole world shrank from. "Let us walk abroad together. I will tell you what I know of me. And you will explain to me all about the night."

They went downstairs and entered the darkness. They walked the length of the street, crossed the canal, and made for the center of town. She gave him the story of her life, talking easily and freely, as if he were no more than a stranger come from far away to settle here. He hung on every word she spoke. He was so delirious with joy that a hundred years of agony was lifted from his heart. They walked through the fallen leaves in the public garden, trailed through the harbor square and out along the pier. She wove a spell from the bits and pieces of her simple life. The night sped away like a dream.

She urged him to say as much for himself, and in a halting voice, he spoke of the man he used to be, centuries before. Then about the castle and the curse. It began as a fatal blood disorder. They called in a doctor who was mad, who fed him the blood of bats to cure him. In a year, his life was no longer in his control. He had caught the hunger for human blood. He spoke, thought Lucy, as if he had never told the tale before.

Miles and miles they walked, through every quarter of the town. And in the end they came, as if by chance, to the dark mass of Red Oaks. The sky had already lightened into gray, some time ago. The dawn was only moments off.

"Won't you come in and rest?" he asked. So dazzled was he for love of her, he seemed to forget that his house was vile and broken and overrun with rats. He had so far lost himself that he seemed to feel she would come in and bed down with him now, pulling up the lid to cover them both.

"Not yet," she said, disengaging herself from his arm. "Give me one more day. Tomorrow night you shall have your answer."

The horizon burned to loose the ray of sun that would destroy him, but he stayed one moment more to take his leave.

"What you call love," he said, "is but a shadow of what could be. Try to think of a love that has a thousand thousand years to grow in. Can you? Oh, Lucy, this one night alone has been worth the time I've waited." He walked up the battered stairs with difficulty, shading his eyes with his hand. When he turned at the door to raise the other hand in parting, he looked so much like a man, no one would ever have known. The suffering that twisted his face was gone. "I will sleep with your picture resting on my heart. Dearest Lucy, choose the night."

And he was gone. She stood in the street, begging the sun to finish rising. Her own heart was full of confusion, but she clung to her mission still. She heard the awful scream from deep inside the house. Another second, and the sun would strike. But then she heard a whirring of wings, and looking up, she saw a bat with a wingspan two feet wide fly up out of the chimney. It sailed away across the rooftops. Gone as the first light made her squint. He'd got away.

And now there was only one way left.

Eight

THE morning dawned sere and terrible in Wismar. Everything had gone wrong. Nothing was still in its place. A herd of cattle from one of the outlying farms came thundering over the bridge of the main canal and barreled its way to the market square. They crashed around in the looted shops and beat their hooves among the broken stalls on the pavement. They seemed to want revenge on the merchants, but time was swift and hard. They began to have fits and convulsions, bumping against each other in the blindness of their pain. And as the carcasses fell and littered the square, the rats came out of the walls to feast. Soon the place was raw and pointless as a battlefield, the only sounds the tear of flesh and the gnashing of teeth. It went on and on, till it seemed a million rats had swarmed the herd. And when there was nothing left but bones, the rats receded like a tide, back to their other work in the fallen town. All across the market square, the bones were white and clean.

The fever had reached the second stage—delirium, sudden paralysis, pain in the guts like disembowelment, foaming at the mouth. Men bit out their tongues and tore at their stomachs. Only the strongest could survive it. The rest died off like flies in a killing frost. The death-boats plied the still canals, picking up corpses lifted out of the waterside windows by the weeping survivors of a household. At the confluence of the waters, a train of coffin-bearers, all in black, put the dead in boxes and bore them on their shoulders to the charnel house at the graveyard gates. The undertaker stood in his icy room and screamed, begging it all to stop. And up and down each street, the coroner went knocking. He chalked one door in four, by noon one door in three. A kind of mercy seemed to attend his passing.

At the hospital, Doctor van Helsing couldn't concentrate. The mad in their cells beneath him had been singing a song all morning. In unison they chanted: "Master, come release us." The doctor went back and forth between his laboratory and his office. He examined a group of corpses that were punctured at the jugular and bloodless in the veins. He had spread open on his desk every book he could find on plague, and he tried to prove scientifically that rats were responsible for these strange deaths. He made measurements and hypotheses. On the bell curve of the research, he took the extreme condition in every case. But he could not make his data fit anything but superstition and nightmare.

Still he would not believe it. His whole life's work had come to naught if the tales of desperate men were the proven truth. Yet he knew he had to speak with Lucy once again, because everyone else in Wismar raved and married chaos. He looked about sadly at all the accumulation of method and reason that hallowed his office, and he knew he was only one against the mob. As he went along the corridor, he could hear the guards and nurses rutting in the sickrooms. Half his staff was crazed with fever, and they took greater and greater pleasure in beating away the pleading victims from the hospital doors. The doctor had no real authority anymore. He waited to care for the survivors, but he had a sinking feeling in his heart that they would only be a pitiful few, and he wondered if the world they would come back to was worth surviving for.

He made his way across the harbor square and entered the streets of the town. Two small boys rode on the back of a sheep. At a cooking fire built on the curb, a ragged man tried to roast a live pigeon. The bird, its feathers singed away, ran out of the fire moaning plaintively, and the madman grabbed it up and thrust it in again, till his own hands were blistered and charred. The doctor crossed the central canal, and there on the bridge, a rich man merrily counted his money into the water, bill by bill. At the other end of the bridge, another man beat on a drum with a white bone. There was a sort of carnival air abroad in the town today, as if, at the pitch of death, the horror had opened the gates to a lawless slapstick.

Outside the old hotel, a cluster of urchins played hide-and-seek in a pile of lacquered furniture and damask drapes. A man with sores all over his face was wearing a horse costume—the rear half of it anyway. He drank a long draught of claret out of a wineskin, and then, as the doctor passed, he let out a long whinney of laughter. The doctor looked over. His eyes widened in disbelief when he saw that the carcass was real. The rats had eaten their fill, and the man crawled into the corpse as if he could change his fate and run away on ringing hooves. Van Helsing knew, as he hurried along, that no plague had ever so dehumanized a people. The maniacal laughter of men in the streets mocked his love of reason. Nuns flagellated each other on the convent steps. A man sold a tulip to a corpse. The foaming policeman arrested a goat. All of them told him his science had come to an end.

When he reached the Harkers' house, he hammered on the door like a man desperate to be awakened from a dream of death. When Lucy appeared, very pale and weary, he clasped her hand and wept as he spoke her name.

"Oh, Lucy, tell me it's not too late," he pleaded. "I am a blind and godless man. Say there is something I can do."

She nodded disconsolately and stood aside for him to enter. She led him into the parlor and pointed across at Jonathan, stirring restlessly in his sleep. Van Helsing went to the sofa, knelt and took the pulse. The man was burning with fever, but the blood still pumped and fought and held its own.

"What I need to know," she said in a tragic voice, "is when you think he'll die. Can he last through another night?"

"I don't know," van Helsing replied, "but there is strength enough here for us to hope. He may be one of the lucky ones. He is halfway there. If he passes the night and another day, he will be through the crisis."

"No," she corrected. "By dawn tomorrow, it will be all over. Those who make it through this night will be saved. Unless I fail. If that should happen, there is no hope for anyone."

She seemed relieved to hear the doctor give her husband better than half a chance. She wandered into the morning room, to her old protected place at the window above the canal. He followed her in and watched as she picked up her needlework, stared at it pathetically, and tossed it aside on the window seat. For a moment, as the silence grew between them, the doctor thought he would not alarm her with news of the horrors he had seen in his journey crosstown. But he realized, watching her staunch and clear-eyed profile, that she had seen it all herself and gone beyond it.

"Do you believe me now?" she asked him. There

wasn't a trace of arrogance or righteousness in her voice.

"I do," he said. "There is a thing more monstrous than the plague in Wismar."

"Then yes," she said, looking up at him gravely, "I *do* have a favor to ask of you. It is not easy, Doctor —or, I should say, it is not *nice*. I want you to promise me this—you will come to my bed at dawn tomorrow and see if I am still alive. If not, if I seem dead, you must drive a stake here"—and she thumped her breast with the flat of her hand—"right into my heart."

His mouth dropped open in terror as he whispered: "Woman, what are you saying?"

By way of an answer, she picked up the book—his very own—from the table by her chair, turned to a page she'd marked with a velvet ribbon, and gave it over into his hands. A passage had been circled, and he read the words like a call of doom: "If a woman pure of heart should make him forget the cry of the cock, the first light of day will destroy him forever."

"Promise me!" she beseeched him.

"But there must be another way!"

"None," she assured him, shaking her head, so they wouldn't waste any time on pipedreams. They stared at one another then, and even Dracula would have had to say they were realists. They knew how little chance she had against the tide of darkness. There was no certainty that van Helsing would get to her in time. Perhaps the vampire would seize her and flee, and she would be trapped forever in the violet light of the Undead. But somebody had to do it, and it was better for her to go into it if she could without illusions. She had to accept it: this was probably her last day on earth.

"Whatever you say, my child," conceded the doctor gently. "And I will promise you one other thing—the people of Wismar are going to know who made this scarifice for them. They will praise your good name forever!"

"No, no," she said, "it doesn't matter. I have had so much love already. I didn't even realize, till all of this began. Jonathan and I lived for a while in a world where we walked as gods. For having that, I owe life something in return. You mustn't feel sorry for *me*."

He hated to leave her. Hated to go back out to the violence and madness that riddled the town. But he knew she needed time to compose herself and put her affairs in order. He was too overcome with emotion to say goodbye. And though he would dearly have loved to ask her why it had come to pass, so much misery and doom, he began to see the shadow of a reason, all on his own.

"Until tomorrow, then," he said, when she'd shown him to the door. "I will come and wake you early, so you shan't miss a moment of the morning."

"And I shall make your breakfast, Doctor," she told him, laughing all the while to hide her fear. "We will eat like kings tomorrow morning."

The day passed all too quickly. Most of the time, she sat by Jonathan's side in the parlor, stroking his fevered brow. He had ceased to rave in his sleep, as if he had told all the story that could fit into words. Whenever he stirred and broke through to consciousness, she fed him milk and toast, though he'd developed the plague victim's revulsion for food. He was painfully thin and pale, and he surfaced with a wounded look on his face, as if he felt betrayed by his own body.

But there were moments, two or three that day, when he looked upon Lucy's tender countenance and came all the way back to the life they shared. Hardly a word would pass between them then, yet they gazed in each other's eyes and renewed the indestructible bond they'd made the day they married. She remembered it all so clearly. They stood outside the chapel, the blossoms of a cherry tree raining down upon them, and Jonathan turned and said: "I promise you, Lucy, our life will be as happy as a dream." And so it had been.

Toward the middle of the afternoon, he struggled to speak. She gave him a sip of water, and then he whispered: "If only we'd known how much we had. It has all fled away from us, Lucy. I should have kissed you more."

"Don't grieve, my darling," she said. "We had it then, and we know it now. More we cannot ask. I love you better in the present hour, dark though the world around us grows, than ever I have before. Now is all we have, and now is more to me than a thousand kisses."

"I will love you forever," he swore to her, tears in his eyes, "no matter if time itself should stop." And he took her hand in both of his and slipped back into a peaceful sleep.

It must have been after three—the sun was shining sidelong through the naked branches of the trees —when she heard a commotion in the street outside. She went to the door and opened it wide, fearful of nothing the daylight had to offer. At the house opposite, two well-dressed gentlemen were carrying a sofa down the steps of a house whose door was marked with a white cross. They were stealing from the dead. They already had a pushcart piled high with booty. In spite of herself, Lucy hurried across the street to berate them.

"What are you doing, you fools? Why are you stealing *now*?" They stopped dead in their tracks and stared at her. She could see they were wild with fever. "Don't you understand," she begged them, "the plague is your redemption. You are free at last of all possessions. Let the rats *have* your houses! Let them sit in your armchairs and sleep in your beds. Tomorrow you must begin to live without these props. The world will be utterly naked again."

But they looked at her quite as if *she* were the one all crazed with fever. They shouldered her aside and heaved their sofa up on the pile. They went away arguing what was whose, pushing their cart to the next house chalked with death. Lucy hurried back across the street and shut herself in. She saw it did no good to act the prophet. They would wake to the new world and see for themselves, or they would die with the old world in the night. Yet she wept for an hour, all alone at the window above the canal, for all those men who clung to the past like a dying animal. She could not hate them. No more than she could hate the vampire, who struggled with an agony all his own. Hate had made no headway in her heart. She'd banished it long since.

It was coming close on dusk when she went and fetched her jewel cask. She walked to the sofa where Jonathan slept in the parlor. She lifted the lid and took up a handful of consecrated wafers. She crumbled them up and dropped them like a trail, in a narrow circle around the place where he would sleep the night. He groaned and struggled as if it were a cage, but she did not stop till she was done. She bent over and examined her work with meticulous care, making sure there was no break in the circle. When he was all protected, she sat by his side a final time, smoothing his forehead with the cool of her hand till he quieted down again.

"Good night, dear Jonathan," she said, her voice breaking. "Be happy, won't you? I do not know when I will see you again, but I go with your face imprinted on my heart. I will not forget you, no matter where the darkness leads me."

He did not hear a word of it, nor did he feel the tear that fell upon his cheek. She wiped it away as if it were some final sorrow she could bear alone. She rose and went away without a backward look, lest she falter in her resolve. She climbed the stairs in the gathering twilight. She came into her bedroom and lit the candles in the sconces, though the glow did not serve to warm her as it used to. She clapped her hands to shoo the cat out of the room, but it left at its own pace, slow as a creature spellbound.

Passionlessly, she stood at the mirror and took off her clothes. She folded each thing neatly and put it in the proper drawer, as if there was something safe in keeping all the order that she could. When she was naked, she cast an indifferent glance at her frail and fully human body. There was no vanity in her. She wore this body as a weapon now, and nothing more. She could scarcely recall the girl who used to study her skin for blemishes and fret about a tooth she thought looked crooked, who wept with rage if she couldn't comb a stray curl from her marvelous hair. The mirror had nothing to show her, least of all herself.

She went to the window and looked out into the the dark. There were bats wheeling in the air above her garden. The rats moved by in procession along the edge of the canal. Though there were no wolves within a hundred miles of Wismar, she could hear a howling close as the neighbor's house. The denizens of the night made ready to adore her. They gathered in endless audience, as if the word had spread that they would have a queen at last. There seemed to be a babble of voices rising on the air. They chanted her damnation, and she did not flinch to hear it. The clock on the church tower chimed, with long resounding echoes.

It's time, she thought as the chimes mounted to midnight, *finally it's time.* She was possessed by the strangest feeling of impatience, like someone condemned at the gallows who wants the ceremony finished, who waves away the priest so as to get it all over with now. The twelfth bell rang, and she felt a wave of power course through her with a murderous desire. She turned to the ground of her sacrifice.

Dracula was already there, waiting inside the door. They had no need to take each other's measure anymore. She did not have to speak her answer. She walked across the room to her bed, and she drew back the linen counterpane as she had a thousand nights before. She lay back among the pillows, her dark hair spread out wantonly. For a moment of awesome stillness, the world seemed to hold its breath. The vampire didn't move. Could it be the dread and modesty had fallen to him? She looked more ready than he was. Seemed to know more how the night would go.

He came to her soundlessly and knelt beside the bed. He put out his hands to touch her, then let them fall to his sides, as if they were not worthy of the whiteness of her flesh. His lip curled up, and his fangs shone dully in the candlelight. She turned her face slightly away as he moved forward, so as to give him the full expanse of her throat. For hundreds of years he'd approached a victim swiftly, puncturing at the neck with an expert speed, without preliminary exploration. But this he came to lingeringly. The razor teeth touched flesh and held a long moment before he made the incision. An unbearable tension of forces gathered to act.

And when the flesh first tore, the cut was so small that only a single drop of blood came beading out. It was weighted like a teardrop, and he drank it like a rare elixir. His body shuddered with glory. He took it drop by drop for what must have been an hour. He hunched like a man praying. Lucy stared off into the light of a single candle, conscious still, and thought it did not hurt at all. She felt a kind of numbness in her throat, twin to the numbness that gripped her heart and would not ever let him enter. She could almost pretend it wasn't happening. She could see Jonathan's face as clearly as she hoped she would. It covered her mind like the summer sky.

Later—neither could say how long—he let the fangs sink into the vein and began to drink, but ever so slowly still. She felt it like a burning at first, and she groped the air with her hand as if to plead with him to stop. He caught up her hand in his and gathered it to his cloak to comfort her. She could feel the beating of his heart like a bell tolling. Then she ceased to struggle. The numbness spread out from her neck, all the way down her arm to the hand he held. She felt herself falling, but not into sleep. She was sure she would never sleep again.

It was more a state of suspension that she entered —as if this moment would go on forever, no matter what else should ever come to follow it. She began to wave in and out of visions, but through all of it, she never lost control. She had so little fear that she decided to explore this part like a cave. The more she could bear to see firsthand, the more likely it was she would beat him in the end. So she entered the incalculable night.

Black bats beat their wings in the darkness, rising out of the nightmare like herons off a marsh. Their mouths were opened wide, but all their cries were soundless. They lived in a great cathedral, far away on a moor, and the god who blessed it once was long forgotten. They kept a vigil in a night without end, waiting for their queen. She was walking down the aisle in a white dress, toward a broken altar. The cross was gone. The chalice was gone. Only the Bible remained, but when she turned the page, the word that blazed like a tongue of fire was *Nosferatu*.

She was on a dark ship that sailed the canals of Wismar. But as it passed under a bridge, it went underground. On either side, gigantic spiders tested the air with their feelers, then reared back and groped with two front legs. A creature like a crab filled the

tunnel in front of the ship, and as they went beneath
his twitching legs, his dead eyes rolled, and she felt
the shell slide over her skin. The tunnel went on and
on, till she became aware of men lined up in a row on
the stone bank. They were still as mummies, and
their mouths gaped open.

Everything in the night was hungry, and yet the
further she traveled into it, the more she saw they
could not prey on her. The corpses leaned against the
walls, exhausted and alone. Their clothes were tat-
tered, and their flesh fell off them like wax along a
candle. They stood frozen in unfinished gestures, not
living and not quite dead. She sailed by them like a
ghost, and she knew that if they reached to touch her,
their hands would catch hold of nothing but the air.
She saw, as never before, how precarious was the
vampire's grip on life. Dracula had crawled somehow
to the lip of the cave, where he hung by a single
thread, and all the hellish world beneath him tried to
pull him back.

When was it, deep in the night, that she felt him
crying as he drank? She put her arms around his neck
and drew him ever closer. She opened her lips and
and made a hushing sound. She wondered how he'd
ever thought he had the power to bring her down with
him. She knew the life was going out of her, but she
had no fear of death, and now there was no chance
that he could detain her, here among the Undead. It
required a cast of mind she simply didn't possess—a
sense of secrecy and guilt, of longing without a name,
of terror to live in time.

The candles had guttered and gone out by the time
the church clock struck four. The vampire barely
breathed. The fangs held on in the vein, but for the
longest time he took nothing in. It was too exquisite
to dream of all that was left, like a pool as deep as the
world, just his alone. He did not hear the panic of
his children, thronging out in the night. They groaned

and howled and pleaded for him to make an end of it and bring her to the kingdom. His hands had begun to roam her body as it cooled and hovered on the brink of death. He had the whole of eternity to keep her by his side, but he knew there would never again be a night like this. For once he was more alive than not. He savored the stroke of time like an open window letting in the moon.

And though she was far gone now, and deeply under his spell, she was crouched in the corner of her mind where the air was free of phantoms, and she counted every minute like a nun at her rosary. A half hour more. She heard the rage of the powers of darkness, moaning at the windows and calling warnings. She was not sure the house could stand up, with the furies bearing down like a hurricane. But she held his head and stroked the pulses in his skull and met him trance for trance. They were so entwined, so locked to a single fate, that there ceased to be any difference between her pain and his. They seemed to lie here like mirrors set face to face, excluding all the world besides. She had half a mind to go with him, flee this sorrowful trap of mortal life forever. And it only made her count the minutes harder.

The vampire heaved a sigh that broke a thousand hearts. He lifted away from her neck, and the look in his eyes was full of dreams. He saw the first light of day as if he didn't understand the significance of it. The rising sun had caught the tip of the tallest steeple in Wismar, and the high gables of the houses at the eastern end of town were bathed in a reddish light. An ominous silence had fallen on the landscape as the creatures of the night withdrew to their lairs. Their final warning didn't even reach him. He had forgotten himself—he who endured five hundred years of knowing nothing else, night after night.

A cock crowed out in the morning air. Another, and then another. The sun lit up the topmost branches of the blighted trees. He made as if to rise, by instinct only. He couldn't see why he should not stay here, where he thought he had come to life again. Her hands around his neck restrained him, so he moved to disengage them. But she moaned so pitifully then, as he tugged to pull away, that he made his fatal error. He looked into her eyes.

There was hardly a breath left in her, and she was whiter than the pillows where she lay, but she gathered all the force still grappling after life and whispered this command: "Take me with you, Master. Do not leave me here alone!"

And he knew he could not go without her. But he had to finish every drop of blood that beat inside her before he could carry her to his bed. He bent again to her neck, bit in, and sucked with a deep abandon. Her eyes were mad with pain as she stared at the brightening window. *Please,* she begged the dawning day. She could not last another second.

A ray of the sun streaked in. It touched the tip of his shoulder and glanced away to a patch of wall. He fell from her, writhing as if a spear had lodged in the bone. He turned in rage, his mouth widened to a rictus and wet with gore, his eyes glazed with vengeance. But it wasn't an enemy he could take and ravage. It was only the sun, and it grew and grew till it flooded the room, because it could not help itself. He caught at his own throat as the breath froze in his lungs. He stood, and it seemed he was going to throw himself through the window, to stop the torture blistering his skin like white-hot bars of iron.

But he was only drawing the drapes. It did no good, of course. The light was all over the room by now. Yet he was frantic to dim the room, even as he choked and plummeted to death. He backed against the foot of the bed and spread his cape to shield his queen. For that is what he was trying to do—save *her*, though he had to die himself. He gave her one last agonized look over his shoulder. He did not seem to have the least idea that she had tricked him to his fate. His eyes were great with sorrow, as if he thought he'd failed her.

She saw it was over at last. She was all but dead as she stared at him, but she was too good, or she understood him now too well, to let him die in such despair. She smiled as if to say the night was magic. His own face lit with triumph, and though he fell, his last thought as he slipped away to his final sleep was this: he had tasted love like any other man.

He lay in a heap on the floor, released from his ancient prison. Lucy looked into the sun. The sky outside her window was bright with the constant image of the man she loved. She had kept it like a faith. She moved her lips to speak his name. *I love you always,* she whispered, a smile of perfect mildness breaking on her face. And the light went out.

All over Wismar, the people woke in the bloom of health. Scores had died in the night, but the fever vanished at the stroke of dawn. Everyone's temperature dropped to normal. The pink came back to their cheeks. The world, or what was left of it, was saved. They sent up what prayers they could still remember to the wide and cloudless heavens, and then they went to work to bury the dead and clear the streets. The rats had disappeared from all the crevices and alleyways. Like brave survivors everywhere, the citizens of Wismar emerged from their houses into the sun and put the horrors of the past behind them. When they saw the littered thoroughfares and plundered shops, they felt no shame because shame would not help them. They cleaned things as best they could and faced the future boldly.

Jonathan didn't at first know where he was. He opened his mouth to call for the Mother Superior, eager to get on his horse and go, but then he realized

169

that part was already finished. He felt a curious sense of anticlimax, seeing he was home. He stood up from the horsehair sofa and tried to step into the room, yet he could not move forward. An invisible wall seemed to cage him in. He sat down again, bewildered, and tried to think what to do.

The front door opened. Jonathan's heart leapt up, to think someone had come to release him. But Doctor van Helsing did not even acknowledge his presence. He made straight for the stairs, glassy-eyed and bent with grief, and in one hand he carried a hammer, in the other a wooden stake. As he mounted up to the bedroom, Jonathan was filled with panic. He stood again and began to scream.

"Help!" he cried, as if a monster had broken in. "Stop him! Somebody stop him!"

And out in the street, the neighbors turned from their cleanup work and started forward to the Harker's house. In truth, they were all irritated to hear the shouting. They felt they ought to maintain a dignified quiet as they brought things back to normal, yet they knew they could not ignore the cry of a man in trouble. They clustered about the doorway, twenty in all perhaps, and a few men ventured in to see what they could do.

"Upstairs!" shrieked Jonathan, standing helplessly in the parlor. He clutched his chest and felt each blow of the hammer as if he were being stabbed himself. "Van Helsing has murdered my wife!"

The men drew back in horror, wishing with all their might that they could call him mad and go back to their work. But they could not turn from the sight that met their eyes. The doctor appeared at the head of the stairs, a bloody hammer in his hand. Jonathan shrieked revenge, and two men hurried up and collared him. A third ran into Lucy's room, came staggering out, and confirmed with a heavy nod that it was so.

"But wait," the doctor pleaded, raising his voice to be heard above Jonathan's threats and accusations. "I have acted to save her soul. She has risked damnation for the rest of us, and death is all she asked for in return. You must let me explain."

But he was just another raving madman, and they sent him sprawling and dragged him from the house. They would lock him up in his own asylum. The neighbors poured in. To give the others an excuse, a couple went over to comfort the grieving husband while a dozen rushed up to see the madman's work. They grouped around the bed and gasped to see her naked, with the stake deep in her heart. And they hurried away to spread the news in the town.

But how could they neglect to see the vampire too, heaped in the corner and dead as a post? Had he vanished the instant he died, shriveled to nothing like ice in the sun?

The neighbor women begged poor Mr. Harker to tell them what they could do. Hadn't they always known that Lucy would turn out bad? They were terribly understanding. When he sent one off to fetch a broom, she went without hesitation. He was all upset about the dust in the parlor, and they knew it was the wage of grief, to attend to minor matters. They bustled about the room, neatening all the disarray, and when the broom was brought, they swept the crumbs from around his bed. He bounded out into the room.

"My horse!" he cried. "I must be off!"

They looked at one another then. They knew the Harkers kept no horse. What was he doing, leaving at a time like this? But he wouldn't stay to give an answer. He ran to the door, looked back strangely up the stairs, but would not go and see. He fled from the house, and the neighbor women shook their heads. They saw he could not bear the shame.

He ran through the streets. The coroner still went from house to house, chalking doors where no one came to answer. The death-boats made their final rounds along the still canals, taking on the victims of the night. But nobody seemed to notice all of that. Wherever Jonathan passed, the people of Wismar called and waved as they cleaned the town and made it the way it used to be.

At the far end of the last bridge, a riderless horse was waiting, stamping his foot and snorting, wild to be on his way. Jonathan crossed the last canal and leapt up into the saddle. They galloped away without a backward look. Bound across the blighted plains. Bound for the steepest mountains. There was something there that he'd only caught the glimmer of. He could not recall a single thing about it, but he knew now, down to the last shred of his being, that it had to be a better world than this. His cloak flew up behind him, whipping in the wind like a pair of wings. Though he had all the time in the world, he hurtled along at a crazy speed. There was so much work yet to be done.

THE BIG BESTSELLERS
ARE AVON BOOKS

☐	The Human Factor Graham Greene	41491	$2.50
☐	The Insiders Rosemary Rogers	40576	$2.50
☐	Oliver's Story Erich Segal	42564	$2.25
☐	The Thorn Birds Colleen McCullough	35741	$2.50
☐	Chinaman's Chance Ross Thomas	41517	$2.25
☐	Kingfisher Gerald Seymour	40592	$2.25
☐	The Trail of the Fox David Irving	40022	$2.50
☐	The Queen of the Night Marc Behm	39958	$1.95
☐	The Bermuda Triangle Charles Berlitz	38315	$2.25
☐	The Real Jesus Garner Ted Armstrong	40055	$2.25
☐	Lancelot Walker Percy	36582	$2.25
☐	Snowblind Robert Sabbag	44008	$2.50
☐	Catch Me: Kill Me William H. Hallahan	37986	$1.95
☐	A Capitol Crime Lawrence Meyer	37150	$1.95
☐	Fletch's Fortune Gregory Mcdonald	37978	$1.95
☐	Voyage Sterling Hayden	37200	$2.50
☐	Humboldt's Gift Saul Bellow	38810	$2.25
☐	Mindbridge Joe Haldeman	33605	$1.95
☐	Polonaise Piers Paul Read	33894	$1.95
☐	The Surface of Earth Reynolds Price	29306	$1.95
☐	The Monkey Wrench Gang		
	Edward Abbey	40857	$2.25
☐	Jonathan Livingston Seagull		
	Richard Bach	34777	$1.75
☐	Working Studs Terkel	34660	$2.50
☐	Shardik Richard Adams	43752	$2.75
☐	Anya Susan Fromberg Schaeffer	25262	$1.95
☐	Watership Down Richard Adams	39586	$2.50

Available at better bookstores everywhere, or order direct from the publisher.

AVON BOOKS, Mail Order Dept., 224 West 55th St., New York, N.Y. 10019

Please send me the books checked above. I enclose $_____ (please include 50¢ per copy for postage and handling). Please use check or money order—sorry, no cash or C.O.D.'s. Allow 4-6 weeks for delivery.

Mr/Mrs/Miss _____

Address _____

City _____ State/Zip _____

BB 3-79

AVON THE BEST IN BESTSELLING ENTERTAINMENT